PRAISE FOR CHARLES AUSTIN MUIR

"Charles Austin Muir might be one of my favorite new authors. *This is a Horror Book* is as silly as it is scary."

— DANGER SLATER, AUTHOR OF *I WILL ROT WITHOUT YOU & HE DIGS A HOLE*

This book is so packed full of bloodshed, mayhem, dream logic, horror movie references, magic spells, hip-hop and weird sex that I don't know what else you could possibly want."

— SCOTT COLE, AUTHOR OF *TRIPLE AXE* AND *SLICES: TALES OF BIZARRO AND ABSURDIST HORROR*

One of the hardest tasks an author has is finding a voice that's distinctly his own, with no apologies to anyone else's use of words or language. Charles Austin Muir has found his. *This is a Horror Book* is a life-mosaic in words, touching on common experience and the unreal, all written with the voice of a sly trickster by a fine horror author who's come into his own."

— C. COURTNEY JOYNER, AUTHOR OF *NEMO RISING* AND THE *SHOTGUN* WESTERN SERIES AND SCREENWRITER/DIRECTOR WITH CREDITS INCLUDING *PRISON*, *CLASS OF 1999* AND *TRANCERS 3*

THIS IS A HORROR BOOK

CHARLES AUSTIN MUIR

CONTENTS

PREVIOUSLY PUBLISHED

"Skype Me at the Public Library" (under the title "Barbee") *Forest of Sex and Death* (2017)

"Catch You on the Flip Side" *CLASH Magazine Issue No. 1* (2018)

"O Mother Goddess, Where Art Thou?" *Strange Behaviors: An Anthology of Absolute Luridity* (2018)

"The Raekwonomicon" *This Book Ain't Nuttin to Fuck With* (2017)

THIS IS A HORROR BOOK

This story is about what happens when two drunk guys get their hands on an evil book on Halloween. Quite possibly, you'll get to the end and tell me, "Charles, you're either full of shit or writing bad social satire."

My response would be one, screw you for being harsh. And two, these events really happened, so you can't call it satire. I saved the world and someone out there who looks like Charlize Theron knows it. Speaking of the actress, that's where this story starts—with me having sex (not really, but sort of) with Charlize Theron. In fact, all good stories start with Charles Austin Muir, writer, hip-hop artist and unsung hero, giving Charlize Theron the D.. I know that sounds delusional, not to mention ungentlemanly to brag about such things, but this shtick has a purpose. More about that later.

Anyway, I was buying taquitos at my neighborhood Sticky Mart store when the disclaimed sex with Charlize Theron took place. Or I should say, I was slowly being bored to death because the credit card terminal wouldn't read my card. To block out Greek John, the possibly autistic clerk, mumbling at the machine from behind the counter, I pictured myself having gland-to-gland combat with Theron as Imperator Furiosa in *Mad Max: Fury Road*. In the back seat of her 18-wheeler, the soldier rode me cowgirl-style while her driver dodged *Cloverfield*-size sandstorms in a post-apocalyptic Australian outback.

"Do me, Charles," Furiosa commanded. "Ride my fury road. Yes… yes… oh, hell yes. Give it to me. Do it. Do it. Do it." And I did all right, all the while sucking on her prosthetic hand made from vise-grip pliers and other items you can get at Home Depot in case you're into cosplay. "Put the number in," she added. Her voice went from cooing to death metal growly. "Put the number in."

"Huh?"

"Put the number in."

Greek John breathed what smelled like fish stock in my face. "Put the number in."

"Oh, yeah. Sorry."

I entered my PIN on the keypad. Suddenly, my beef-and-pepper-jack taquitos seemed lame compared to knocking motor-cycle boots with Furiosa.

Greek John death metal growled, "Have a nice day," and recycled my receipt. I really wished Lebanese John would get back on the day shift. My customer satisfaction mattered more than his sick child.

Kidding. But I'm not kidding when I say I turned the corner of the building and saw a book propped against the brick wall. To call it a book doesn't do it justice. It was more like a strongman implement bound in reddish-brown leather with metal clasps and studs that made it look as though it hovered off the ground. Not your typical reading material left on the side-walk with a "free" sign on it. This was one heavyweight, medieval-looking tome.

No homeless people had staked out the environs, so I knelt on the cement walkway and gave the book close inspection. I'm no expert, but the thing looked real-deal historical. Everything from the cracks on the spine to the buckling of the page edges to the faded gold tooling screamed authenticity. This thing looked *organically weathered*, and I know you can replicate that, but it had an aura too that made me feel out of my time just looking at it.

So why was the book propped up outside a Sticky Mart?

Was it a history professor's curb alert item? A prank? God forbid, a booby trap? I tilted the tome a few inches from the wall. I didn't see anything behind it, no wires or biohazardous substances, nor did I detect suspicious odors. I glanced around. What the hell, I thought. I got to my feet and hoisted the book like a barbell. I was now the proud owner of a possible relic from the Middle Ages.

After I peed the dog and ate the taquitos, I set the book on my kitchen table. I sat down and opened the upper and lower clasps. They had been made in the shape of skeleton fingers. When you pulled them back, you revealed a man's face with eyes torn out and mouth open in a scream. Freaking cool... so cool it made me nervous. I mean, other than having clean hands, was there a special way to handle a book like this? Should I Google "handling rare materials?" Then again, I found the manuscript outside a Sticky Mart—why was I suddenly agonizing over touching it? Was I afraid of damaging an irreplaceable piece of history? Or something else?

Perhaps... the book itself?

Pfft, I thought. Or said, because no one thinks in pffts. Everyone knows a book can't literally hurt anyone. Just treat it with care, I told myself. I opened the front board halfway, mindful not to put too much pressure on the joint holding the board to the book. Gently, I leafed through the thousand-plus-page volume. I didn't recognize the language, not surprisingly, so I had no idea what I looked at. Just pages of dense black script as if some remote ancestor of Greek John droned on about how to use an abacus. No pictures or even a splash of color for the child in me. In terms of perusing, this tome kind of sucked.

But as a sensory experience, it really swept me into the gruesomeness of the period. Besides the clasps, the book had real animal skin instead of paper. Parchment, if you're not in the know. The pages were stained and patchy and more yellow than white, with follicles breaking up text and holes where the parchment maker had punctured the skin while scraping animal hair off. Yuck. They crackled when I turned them, too, as if the ghost of the cow or goat or whatever had given up its flesh hated me for reminding it why it had died.

Altogether a creepy effect... and not something that would come across in a picture or video. So rather than flaunt my find on social media, I texted my friend Jay.

That was the first of many mistakes that night.

❀

"Happy Halloween, dude," Jay whispered. Quickly, as if I were a drug dealer or mistress, he shooed me through his front door and turned off the porch light.

He was hiding in his basement because of all the hipsters out trick-or-treating. Judging by his bloodshot eyes and sudden surfer accent, he had also opened a case of beer to lament the hipster-ruined holiday.

He held out a Corona. "Beer ya?"

"Got bourbon in the backpack," I said, but chugged half the beer anyway. In the world of manly drinking, it is an unwritten rule that the visitor must catch up with the host as quickly as possible.

Jay nodded and steered me into the hallway. He didn't want passing hipsters to see us through the door's glass panes. "They can smell when you want to be left alone, dude, I swear it." He shut off the living room lights and took a leak while I went downstairs to his man cave.

I finished the Corona while studying his library. The upper bookshelves contained his parents' literary hand-me-downs and my modest oeuvre. Flattering and kind of funny to see the horror anthologies I'd been in next to *The Oxford Shakespeare* and *Alice's Adventures in Wonderland*. The lower bookshelves held assorted hardcovers Jay got at garage sales. He didn't care so much what these books were about, so long as they looked like they'd gathered dust in an old woman's closet.

When he saw what I had in the main compartment of my backpack, he would flip. But I didn't want to show him right away. I would wait until we finished the movie paused on his sixty-inch flat screen TV: The horror film of choice for all middle-aged men on a beer-fueled movie binge, director Stanley Kubrick's *The Shining*.

In the world of manly movie-watching, it is an unwritten rule that you should never interrupt *The Shining* unless you must pee or process some background detail you had never noticed before.

There is no rule that you cannot look at Facebook, however, as long as you throw out a quote or two at the right moments to show you're at least half-paying attention to Kubrick's unfaithful, conspiracy theory-inspiring adaptation of Stephen King's novel. Which is what we did while we waited for Jack Torrance to chase his son, Danny, through the hedge maze and (spoiler alert —if you're lame enough to have never seen the movie) end up freezing to death.

"July 4, 1921, dude," Jay called out, posting Jack Torrance memes on my Facebook wall. I looked up from my phone in time to see the black-and-white photograph bearing that date at the end of the movie.

"Nice, man." I sipped from the flask of Bulleit I had brought with me. "Hey, before you put something else in, I've got something to show you."

"Something really scary?" Jay was quoting Dan Aykroyd at the beginning of *Twilight Zone: The Movie*.

"Sure." I mean, to the modern mind, pages made from animal flesh might be considered somewhat scary. Come to think of it, maybe the book had been made while the Black Plague went around—that was definitely scary. "Do you have a towel? This thing might be kind of valuable."

"Uh… yeah, dude. Go ahead and put the empties on the floor." Jay tossed his phone on the couch and went upstairs. I could hear him taking a piss in the bathroom on the landing. While he puttered around in the kitchen, I "liked" all the memes he had posted on my Facebook wall. Then I set the ten or so beer bottles he had polished off under the coffee table.

I took another pull on the flask. Though the room was chilly, I felt flushed and mildly claustrophobic.

"All right if I open the window?" I called out.

"Sure, man. Be right down."

I opened the small square window set just above ground level with a view of the street. A minute later, Jay returned with two more beers and a dish towel. He shivered.

"Should I close the window?"

"Nah, I'm good."

He spread the dish towel on the coffee table and threw on a Seattle Seahawks sweatshirt lying on the couch arm. "Beer ya?" He said. I shook my head, burning my insides with more bourbon. I had quite a buzz going. My friend plopped down on the couch beside me, opened a beer and sized up the window. He shot the bottle cap through it by snapping his thumb and middle finger.

"Score, dude!"

"Nice."

"Let's see you do it."

"I can't do that."

"Sure you can."

"I can't do that."

"I ever tell you I love Stevie Nicks?"

I sighed.

I told myself to tread carefully. The thing is, when Jay gets drunk he will tell you at some point that he loves the former Fleetwood Mac singer, Stevie Nicks. I couldn't afford to get side-tracked by Stevie Nicks. What with the alcohol I had mixed fairly quickly, I had enough difficulty locating the zipper tab on my backpack in the light of the main menu on the flat screen TV. On the other hand, I didn't want to offend Jay lest he be unreceptive to my show-and-tell presentation. I said, "She's cool." And found the zipper tab, finally.

"Cool? That's it? Give me your top three Stevie songs."

"I don't know, man. That's a tough one." I reached into the backpack.

"Your number one, then."

"Hey, can you turn on the light behind you? You're going to want to get a good look at this."

"Dude, you've got to have a favorite Stevie song." Jay

reached back and switched on the floor lamp. "For me, it's a toss-up between—"

"Hold on, wait till you see this." Grandiosely, I pulled the manuscript from the backpack and set it on the coffee table.

"What is that?"

"It's a book."

"I can see that." Jay rubbed his chin.

"It's so old it's handwritten," I said proudly. "Like by monks or something."

"Where did you get it?"

"Outside a Sticky Mart."

"Can I... touch it?"

"As long as your hands are dry."

He set his beer around the end of the couch, wiped his hands on his jeans and ran them over the leather binding. Glancing at me for approval first, he opened the clasps. "Wow. Creepy."

"Right? I knew you would appreciate it. I guarantee this is the oldest book you've ever laid eyes on."

Jay tilted his head and peered at the stud sticking vertically from the bottom of the back board. "What's this? Looks like a button in there. You got a pen?"

"Uh, yeah..." I didn't know if I wanted him poking at my treasure, though. Still, I dug a pen from a zippered pocket in my backpack.

He waved it off. "Maybe you better do it." He repositioned the book so I could see into the stud better.

For more concentrated light, I pulled up the flashlight app on my phone and aimed the light at the bottom of the stud. Sure enough, a button was recessed inside it. I hunched down and inserted the tip of the pen cap into the recess. Jay braced the book's head with one hand while I pushed the button with the pen cap.

Click.

A cloud of dust went up from the book and enveloped our heads. For several moments, we stared at each other through the blackish haze like hikers waiting for a distracted bear to walk by. Then the cloud vanished. It left no odor, no coating, no apparent physical effects except a minute shift toward sobriety.

"That can't be good," I said.

"Yeah. But at least now we know what this book is."

"What do you mean?"

"It's a horror book."

"What do you mean it's a horror book?"

"It's a horror book." He nodded at the manuscript, a sort of hybrid puzzle box with a hidden mechanism that unlocked its secrets, apparently.

I shined my phone's light at the bottom of the book block. Where no writing had been, a title indicated in red gothic letters: *THIS IS A HORROR BOOK.*

In the off-chance you write a book report on this story—and remember, it's *nonfiction*—here is the main theme: When two guys get together, their intelligence quotients drop by half. When you give them alcohol and a national reason to watch horror movies, their intelligence quotients drop by another half. When you give them an evil book, their intelligence quotients drop by another half. That doesn't leave much intelligence to spare—but enough to launch doomsday, unfortunately.

And that's what we were about to do, only we didn't have enough intelligence to think of it that way, or think of anything except posting *The Shining* memes on each other's Facebook walls for half an hour. By the way, that's how otherwise heterosexual men often express their true feelings for each other in the digital age: We post movie memes on each other's Facebook walls and react by tapping the "love" button.

But seriously, Jay and I were steeling ourselves for our next experiment with *A Horror Book.* Or with *This is a Horror Book.* Whatever. I'll call the manuscript the horror book.

You see, before our Facebook break, we flipped through the horror book. We discovered it was technically a magician's manual divided into sections on *invoking* and *evoking* supernatural beings. I knew enough about magic to want to avoid *invoking* anything whatsoever. I doubted either of us wanted a demonic entity inside us.

The problem was, the horror book didn't specify what beings you could evoke, or call forth to reality, by speaking its incantations. To give you an idea, here is what we were dealing with (minus the invoking section):

EVOCATIONS

I - Scary Horror
II - Way Scarier Horror
III - Way, Way Scarier Horror
IV - Way, Way, Way Scarier Horror
V- Way, Way, Way, Way Scarier Horror
VI- Super Scary Horror Beyond Imagining
VII – Game Over, Man

Yes, I know those are silly translations. And yes, I realize casting spells requires more work than reciting something. All I can say is the magic dust auto-translated the text in our drunken phraseology, and speaking of drunk, that counts as an altered state at least semi-conducive to magical operations.

Oh, and it's Halloween, remember? And the book works sort of like a puzzle from Hell? We are talking a perfect storm of scary-horror-conjuring.

One more thing: If you're wondering how the book could run longer than a thousand pages, the bulk of each chapter said "words" over and over again. So you had maybe ten pages of unexplained incantations and then "words words words" until the poor scribe felt like moving on to another chapter.

Memed out, and replenished with liquid courage, we put our phones down and opened the book to see which spell we wanted to try out.

"Summon Stevie Nicks," Jay said. Then recalling magic requires precision, he added: "Er... 1979 Stevie Nicks."

"I'm not going over every page to try and find something with Stevie Nicks," I said.

"Well then, just pick something, I guess. In the 'Way Scarier Horror' chapter."

I turned to the chapter. I wiped my hands on my jeans, closed my eyes and put my pointer finger on the page. I opened my eyes. "Gawd... this stuff is worse than Lovecraft. All right, here goes. G'foolahgundkrahk'gadahga!" I shouted.

We looked at each other again like the hikers waiting for the bear to pass them.

"Holy shit!" Jay clapped a hand to his chin, staring over my shoulder.

I turned and saw someone dressed like the *Scream* killer materialize from the 180-gallon aquarium standing in front of the back wall.

The *Scream* guy, holding his knife up, ran from the room, up the stairs and out the front door.

Several *what-the-fucks* and *did-you-see-that-shits* later, we grabbed our phones and scrolled through our Facebook feeds for news of a *Scream* impersonator on the loose. Granted *Scream* isn't as popular as it used to be, still this wasn't exactly a headline-grabber on Halloween night.

Then Jay said, "My friend just posted that a guy dressed in a 'Ghostface' mask stabbed three people at a strip club."

"Is your friend at the strip club?"

"He's a bouncer. He's one of the dudes who got stabbed."

"Oh."

Jay grinned. "You can't let that stop us, though. It's Halloween. Pick another of those—what do you call it—incunabulations."

"Incantations." I sipped my beer. I'd run out of bourbon several Jack Torrance memes ago. "No, it's your turn. Don't go crazy, though."

Jay turned to a page in the next chapter and shouted: "Grkkahg'luglug'jovghad!"

The "Way, Way Scarier Horror" turned out to be a vampire with pointy ears, fangs and long, gnarly hands outstretched like Elvis Presley sparring with an invisible karate instructor. Staring bug-eyed at us, the creature emerged from the aquarium like the *Scream* killer.

"It's Nostradamus, dude!" Jay shouted.

"Nosferatu," I said.

"Does he do predictions?"

"He does blood-sucking."

"I predict he's going to—change into a bat and fly out the window!" The latter detail added as Nostradamus—I mean Nosferatu, changed into a bat and flew out the window.

"Score, dude!" Jay slapped his knee.

I sank back into the couch cushions. Doing sorcery was surprisingly stressful. "I think I'm done," I said.

"Come on, man, we're just getting started. Here, pick something." Jay slid the book toward me. "This is horror, dude. You. Write. Horror. Am I right?"

"I write something like it."

"One more spell, okay? One more—no, two more spells. Then we're done. Okay? Cool. Here, I'll go first."

My drunk friend (I only emphasize that because he was even drunker than me) (also—what anger does to the Hulk's muscles, beer does to Jay's urge to party, or in this case, to cast magic spells) scooted closer to the horror book, turned to a page in the next chapter and shouted:

"Grphlunkn'gnathn'shtupperkunk'n!"

This time, a lidless box of rabbits materialized in front of the aquarium. We rushed over to it and knelt on the carpet.

"This isn't 'Way, Way, Way Scary,'" Jay said, petting one of the rabbits. "This is way way cute."

"Yeah, but you remember *Night of the Lepus*, don't you?"

Jay squinted, calling up the Seventies movie about giant, man-eating rabbits terrorizing a small town in his boozy data bank. "God, you're right."

We clambered to our feet and swayed with dehydration. As

best I could, I grabbed the box of rabbits and tottered to the window.

"Help me get these things out of here!"

"Aw, you can't throw them out like that, dude," Jay said. He reminded me of Lennie from *Of Mice and Men*, but with beer breath and a surfer accent that only comes out when he's sauced. The rabbits grew as he spoke, though. So he got up on the couch and helped me lift the box and toss it through the window. No easy feat with a flimsy, lidless box full of exponentially expanding rabbits, no matter what your state of consciousness.

Now as big as Volkswagen buses, the rabbits stampeded down the street. We listened to their war cries, a medley of gurgling, neighing and roaring noises, fade into the night.

"Your turn, dude," Jay said.

"I got to pee," I said.

"Cool. How about we do one more spell after you come back, and then we'll watch *Salem's Lot*?"

Of course, he would pick a TV miniseries (adapting another Stephen King novel) that ran over three hours. But I didn't argue with him. I had to pee so bad I nearly wet my pants racing to the bathroom on the landing.

"More beers," Jay called up.

Relieved, I grabbed the last two Coronas from the fridge and returned to the basement. The room stank of man sweat and rabbits. I didn't even feel all that drunk anymore, just exhausted. I yawned. "What time is it?"

"Two-thirty-seven." By contrast, Jay seemed more awake than ever. "Like the room in *The Shining*. Hey—a friend posted she saw a vampire-looking dude peeping in her window."

"Really?"

"Really. She lives in an apartment on the fourth floor."

"Whoa. Any other news?"

"Some hot chick 'liked' your Jack Torrance meme."

"Cool, who—never mind, I'll look that up later. Any other news?"

"A group of giant rabbits attacked a homeless camp near Providence Hospital."

"Shit. Really?"

"Really." He put his phone down. "All right, dude, one more spell. Come on, you know you want to. It's Halloween and we're doing some fucked-up shit. We just conjured a bunch of giant rabbits and that means we've officially tumbled down the rabbit hole. I know you've never done drugs, Charles, but trust me when I say this book is the ultimate trip. One more spell. Go for it. Then *Salem's Lot*."

I sighed. I wished I'd never brought the damned horror book to my friend Jay's house.

Fighting to keep my eyes open, I turned to the "Super Scary Horror Beyond Imagining" chapter. I was so tired I didn't notice I'd skipped past the "Way, Way, Way, Way Scarier Horror" chapter. I closed my eyes, put my pointer finger (damp with spilled beer—I didn't care anymore) on the page and looked at the chosen incantation.

"Kghdvbrid'gudie'sgixvlk!" I shouted.

And in case you're wondering, these aren't the actual incantations. They're random key strokes with apostrophes to make the gibberish look more foreign and ominous. I don't remember the actual incantations, thank God.

Honestly, we probably could have made up any old words and the book still would have conjured something from the combined horror knowledge in our memory banks—bearing in mind the drop-off in brainpower when two guys get together, consume alcoholic beverages, watch horror movies and get their hands on an evil book.

Bearing that in mind, you will no doubt predict what happens next in this story.

Boom.

Boom.

Boom.

Bird's-eye view of an evil book lying on a coffee table.

Boom.

Boom.

Boom.

RRRRRRRRWWWWWWGGGGGGGGG

Close-up shot of two sweaty drunk guys sitting on a couch, glancing sideways at each other.

So the *booms* are footfalls and the

RRRRRRRRWWWWWWGGGGGGGGG

is my attempt to spell out the roar of a Super Scary Horror Beyond Imagining while it's wrecking a city. I can't tell you how small it makes you feel when you experience the magnitude of noise produced by trees and cars and houses being smashed or blowing up around you. Unless you've been through a war or something.

And this was war all right, a war to end everything. Yep, you guessed it. By skipping to the next-to-last chapter, I had made the biggest mistake of the night: I had summoned what I call the Clovercraft Monster.

Obviously, something that formidable isn't going to materialize from a 180-gallon aquarium. It's going to emerge full-grown wherever it fucking feels like. Going by direction and how close it sounded, I'm guessing it broke into this dimension near the strip club where Jay's friend works. Rough night for a bouncer. Now maybe two blocks north, the monster sounded like an earthquake, a thunderstorm and Chewbacca looped on a loudspeaker a thousand times more powerful than Jay's Bose surround sound system. Also, you could hear the *pew pew pew* of laser blasts. I wouldn't say that constitutes a super scary horror beyond imagining, but it is different and could destroy the earth in a large enough force.

Our beers finished, we sat on the edge of our seats and watched out the window. The sky lit up with explosions as if we'd magically transported ourselves into an alien invasion movie.

"Holy shit, dude." Jay swung around and grabbed me by the

shoulders. He was sweating profusely. "You go out on the porch, I'll meet you there. This calls for reinforcements. I got to make a detour first." I think he had to poop, but damned if I grasped his plan overall. I nodded though, because in the world of manly strategizing it is an unwritten rule that you must agree to any proposal that lacks a central idea. This is one reason why the patriarchy is slowly killing the world.

I went outside. The fresh air was nice, if you could get past the stink of stuff burning. The ground shook so violently I nearly fell off the porch. Now too thoroughly freaked out to feel drunk or tired, I made it down to the cement path. I grabbed onto the iron gate giving onto the sidewalk and beheld the imaginable but still super scary horror monster.

It was at least four hundred feet high. It walked on four legs and had gray, scaly skin and a forked tail. Its forelegs were longer than its hind legs, with double-jointed hands that allowed it to stump along on its fingers. Along its humped back, tentacles whipped around, uprooting trees and smashing parked cars on top of other parked cars. On top of its head, a biological cannon fired green lasers that made the *pew pew pew* sounds. Finally, because no gigantic monster is complete without an anthropo-morphic trait, it had frown lines to go with its glowing orange eyes so that it looked super-scary pissed. I'd be pissed too if I had extra tentacles hanging from my mouth.

I had no idea what movie this monster came from. I could only guess the book had used my memories to combine the *Cloverfield* monster with Cthulhu, the deity that made H.P. Love-craft synonymous with slithering appendages. Or maybe the book had conjured it from something Jay remembered watching (like, where did the laser cannon come from?). At any rate, the Clovercraft Monster stomped and laser-blasted its way toward our street. Oh, and the whole time I stood gawking, people were fleeing. They wore vintage clothing and funny wigs. Hipsters. Trick or treat, douchebags.

Watching the hipsters running around screaming like extras in a kaiju movie directed by Ed Wood's ghost, I had an epiphany. Okay, not an epiphany... another fantasy. I heard Furiosa

talking dirty to me again inside my head: "Ride my fury road,"
etc. I didn't know anything about her sexuality in the *Mad Max*
universe, but in the Charles Austin Muir universe the thought of
her lusting after me inspired me to do hero things. And that's
what my bragging about Charlize Theron was about at the
beginning—the real or imaginary sexual cheerleading it takes for
a not-so-macho man to step up and do hero things. Call me a
moron, but I was stoked to send the mega-beast to Valhalla when
I turned to go back inside.

Jay stepped onto the porch just then. He joined me on the
cement path and didn't even look at the monster. Instead, he
tapped and swiped his thumb on his phone. "They're every-
where," he said. "New York... London... Tokyo... Istanbul...
Moscow... Paris... Dude, what have you done? The things are
all over the place. It looks like a goddamn town meeting. They're
coming through the goddamn walls. We're in some real pretty
shit now, man. Game over, man. Game over!"

In case you think my friend meant to chew me out, he was
quoting from *Aliens*. In the world of manly self-expression, it is
standard practice to imply rather than express strong feelings by
quoting from *Aliens*. Still, I got his drift—this catastrophe was my
fault. Sure, "Game Over, Man" technically referred to the horror
after the "Super Scary Horror Beyond Imagining" chapter, but
Mr. Super Scary (not to mention his counterparts around the
world) seemed bent on making sure there would be no further
evoking even if Jay and I had wanted to continue.

My friend stared at me as if he wanted to quote from *Aliens*
again.

"Get the book," I said.

"Whah? Are you crazy—"

"Get the book. Do it."

He went inside.

Across the street, the Clovercraft Monster went rhino-raging
on a Douglas fir tree. It weakened the tree with several laser
blasts and charged. Cheater. Meanwhile, a lone hipster in a
marching band jacket ran around it and got cut in half by a
tentacle.

As panicked hipsters dashed past the house, Jay returned with the horror book, huffing and red-faced. "Dude, what are you gonna do?"

I took the tome. "Thanks for being my number one fan, Jay." The man had enjoyed every story I had ever written. My wife couldn't even say that.

His face went slack. "Dude, whatever you're thinking…"

Furiosa. That's what I was thinking. Yes, I'm married (to a strong woman, too—wait till you read "The Haddonfield Hit Squad"), you've got me. At the same time, I can't help that this nonexistent, badass woman from a *Mad Max* movie got my adrenaline pumping—an important ingredient in any recipe for an act likely to result in self-sacrifice.

Aside: If you expect the bottle cap Jay shot through the window to play a part in my stand against the creature, that's a nice idea… but no. It's just a bottle cap.

But to continue, I opened the book to the dreaded *Invocations* section. "Typqke'kgkix'ekmebbo!" I shouted.

Immediately, I had a horrifying vision. But I'll skip ahead to how I threw down against the monster.

First, I handed Jay the horror book. Then, as hipsters shrieked and fell beneath the creature's tentacle assaults and laser blasts, I levitated in the air till I met the Super Scary Horror Beyond Imagining at eye level. High above the carnage, I floated like Storm from the *X-Men* movies but without the psionic ability to manipulate the weather and slammed the beast with the power of my eyes. That's it, people: I tilted my head down and looked at the monster under my eyebrows.

In pop culture circles, this look is called "the Kubrick stare" because Stanley Kubrick has someone do it in all of his movies. Jack Nicholson used it to super creepy effect in *The Shining*.

But to multiply its power five hundred percent, a demon who apparently loved Stanley Kubrick movies had possessed my body and now unleashed the stare with supernatural intensity. Terrified, the monster screamed "Ggwwwrghh" like Chewbacca in deafening surround sound. While it shook with rage and waved its tentacles, Imperator Furiosa once again spoke inside my head: "Do it. Do it. Do it." So I did it. My eyeballs impervious to the strain of upward-staring thanks to the demon, I floated to within a few feet of the monster's frowny, laser-shooting face—and smiled.

With a final "Rrraarrwhhgwwr," the creature vanished.

I descended to Jay's place cement path. Fortunately, the demon vacated me when I landed. Though I'm not entirely sure it left me, because sometimes I still catch myself looking at people with my head tilted down. Anyway, I thanked the demon mentally and waited for mobs of hipsters to parade me through the street. Guess what? They didn't.

One even had the nerve to stop outside the gate and say, "Hey buds, trick or treat." With my back-to-normal human abilities, I Kubrick-stared him. He shrugged and rejoined his group searching for a house party where they could drink Pabst Blue Ribbon. They all wore funny wigs and a lot of the guys wore marching band jackets.

This whole time, Jay had his eyes glued to his phone.

"The monsters have disappeared, dude," he said. "All over the world. How did you do it?"

"You didn't see?"

"See what?"

"Oh, for God's sake." I took his phone.

He was watching a video. Footage of the monster from a minute ago, screaming. I was the one who made it scream. But I wasn't in the video. Apparently, the demonic Kubrick stare is so frightening it renders its wielder invisible to technology.

"You seriously watched the whole thing on your phone?"

"There's some good footage, dude. A bunch of people live-streamed it."

I sighed.

❀

I'll fast-forward through the boring stuff next. The bro hug, the Lyft ride back to my house. The hour on Facebook searching for validation that I had done something selfless for humankind.

Nothing. Dejected and too tired to sleep, I threw on clean clothes, grabbed my backpack and headed to Sticky Mart. After being possessed, levitating and Kubrick-staring a kaiju, I figured I deserved some early-morning taquitos.

Before I treated myself though, I put the horror book back where I had found it. Everyone knows this is the only way to get rid of a cursed book.

As I expected, the evil tome vanished when I propped it against the brick wall. It would no doubt reappear when the next fool came around who wanted to drink and watch horror movies with a friend on Halloween. Well, what could I do about it? I went inside the store. Greek John was pulling a double shift... Oh, wait. I was going to tell you about my horrifying "Game Over, Man" vision before I defeated the Clovercraft Monster.

In my vision, the sky was gray and I stood in a crowd surrounding an overturned car in a field. Everyone, even police and firefighters and paramedics, looked at the wreck with the Kubrick stare. Creepy in its own right. Worse though, were the luminous patterns of text and thumbnail images refreshing on their faces... and the blue navigation bar superimposed on their eyebrows. The crowd reached to the horizon, a sea of tilted-down, Facebook-monitoring faces. Even now, I wonder what the vision was telling me. That I needed a break from social media? Or that someday soon we will be infected by a global, Kubrick-staring techno-plague?

Heavy-handed? I didn't come up with it. That's straight from the horror book, or the demon that possessed me. Not sure which.

So back to Sticky Mart.

Greek John took his time pulling the taquitos from the roller grill. Bone-weary and bummed that no one had seen me levitate, I waited at the counter and wanted to cry. That's right, no *Aliens* quotes to imply my feelings, just straight up cry. No better place than Sticky Mart for a 5 a.m. existential crisis. After all, I had royally fucked up. Nearly annihilated the world. Unleashed a horny *Scream* killer, a Peeping Tom Nosferatu and a herd of giant, homeless-people-eating rabbits. Who does that? Only a dumbass like me, Charles Austin Muir. A middle-aged, mediocre writer and hip-hop artist (*Brown Boyz* sold only four copies, for real) with too much time on my hands and an itch for adventure. I'd scratched my itch, all right—almost at the world's expense. I wanted to throw the towel in, if I'd had any idea what I was fighting for.

Greek John set the bag of taquitos on the counter. I swiped my card. I was struggling to hold back the tears when a woman walked up to me—a dead ringer for Charlize Theron. Even more amazingly, she celebrated the holiday in a costume that nailed Furiosa's desert warrior look. This Furiosa incarnation smiled and stroked my cheek with her thumb made from vise-grip pliers.

Not a spoiler alert: In *Mad Max: Fury Road*, men destroy the world. Women rebuild it. Simple message. And I wholeheartedly agree with it—look at what Jay and I had done with some booze and a book. But right then at the Sticky Mart, Furiosa threw me a bone. She kissed me on the forehead and said, "So a man really can save the world."

Stunned, I watched her walk out the door.

I imagined us in the back seat of her 18-wheeler, Furiosa riding me cowgirl-style while her driver dodged *Cloverfield*-size—

"Put the number in."

"Huh?"

"Put the number in."

"Oh, yeah. Sorry."

Smiling, I walked out of the store, thinking about what Furiosa had said. Granted, I had made many colossal mistakes in the last few hours, but I had done at least one thing right. Even better, one person on the entire planet had witnessed it.

Standing in front of the Sticky Mart, I ate the taquitos. I decided to check Facebook one more time for footage of my world-saving act. Nothing. Jay, however, had posted a meme on my wall showing the vampire boy knocking on the window in *Salem's Lot*.

Good old Jay, my number one fan.

I reacted by tapping the "love" button.

SKYPE ME AT THE PUBLIC LIBRARY

A logical starting point would be to ask: George, how do you know Charles Austin Muir? The answer is, I don't know him. Not really.

I also want to point out I don't care all that much for horror stories.

Oh, I read Stephen King back in high school, and I enjoy watching a horror movie now and then. But I'm more of a nonfiction guy. Not that there's anything wrong with Mr. Muir, it's just that I prefer to figure out ways to help people rather than disturb them. Or gross them out. I was a personal trainer before all this weird shit happened.

My full name is George John Wayne Kuato. I include my middle name (one name, no hyphen) to distinguish me from the George/Kuato twins in the Arnold Schwarzenegger movie, *Total Recall*. You remember Kuato, the telepathic mutant who lived in his brother's belly? Anyway, as much as I enjoyed the original *Total Recall*, I would rather not be confused with George and his mutant brother, Kuato.

Just to be clear: Like Charles Austin Muir, I'm a three-name guy. George. John Wayne. Kuato.

I'm from a small town. For a while I lived in a big city until my mom got sick and I came home to take care of her. This was in the early 2000s. After my mom died, I sold her house, took an apartment and worked for an ex-bodybuilder named Bev. She ran a gym she simply called The Lab.

One of the benefits of my new job included advice from Bev that helped me get bigger and stronger without gaining fat. People noticed my transformation and signed up. The gym did well until the recession hit. Business improved the following year, but not enough to save us from the malaise that struck the town when the yuppies moved closer to the cities where they made their living.

And not enough to save us from the new library.

After the recession, the town looked like it did when I was a kid: Like nobody lived there. Straggly lawns, dead storefronts, deserted streets as though everyone waited for something awful.

The only awful thing to happen was sedentarism. Behind the closed blinds in the houses on every street, you knew people were sitting on their asses watching television. That's how my dad had spent his days off, and how my mom had spent her whole adult life off. With a Pepsi in her hand watching her "stories."

I'm not saying kill your TV. I'm saying lumbar spine degeneration. Acetabular rim degeneration. Meniscal tears, subacromial bursa thickening. This isn't a NFL lineman's MRI I'm talking about, but what's building up in you right now. The natural aging process. I'm saying your life is a presidential election and you want to vote for strong muscles, not physical weakness.

The problem is it's easier to escape. Retreat from your body into some mindless diversion. Close the blinds. Crack open another cold beverage. Flip to your favorite premium cable channel. I don't say this as a fitness snob, but as someone who watched his mother die in her living room in a hospital bed. Escape sets you up for a slow, ugly death. I'd rather go out like they do in Mr. Muir's bizarre horror stories.

So, after the town reverted to its hermit-like ways, The Lab clung to life by the thread of its hardcore members. A close-knit group of mostly older folks who refused to become shut-ins. Bev and I helped them become athletes of everyday life. We believed that if you could deadlift from the floor and box squat with even light weight, then you could carry any reasonable load, reach into any cranny and safely reverse from any position.

Bev said once, "Doing a hip hinge with a barbell on your back is like throwing a sucker punch at mortality."

But you want to know when the weird shit happens, right?

About eight months ago, I'd guess (I honestly have no sense of time anymore), Bev was diagnosed with stage 4 ovarian cancer. It had spread throughout her body. Seven weeks later, she died. She was 66. Before her health declined, she could do fifteen dead-hang pull-ups and bench press 155 pounds. Then refuel, as she liked to say, with her senior discount at Applebee's.

Bev had been sucker punched by the best cheap shot in the business. And she got to watch the gym she'd poured her life into go down with her.

We didn't think much of the new library, at first. We had a good view of it from our front window. The sprawling brick building stood on Bauman's Hill overlooking the main drag. It must have taken at least six months to complete. Of course, to Bev and me, struggling to keep up our little business, the library seemed to have sprung up overnight.

The paper ran a brief on it. According to the article, the library committee—whose members remained nameless—had decided to expand its facilities in hopes of "reinvigorating" the community.

A crowd gathered on the front steps on opening day. The next week, it grew to a casual assembly overflowing the lawn each morning. We got a close look at the people who approached the library by turning off Main Street. They looked confused, bundled in heavy coats, some in pajamas, dragging themselves toward the hill like nursing home escapees who had some vague idea they were going home.

Still, that was a good thing, right? The library committee had succeeded. The new facility was drawing the troglodytes from their caves. Except the library became their new cave… a catacomb to haunt daily from opening to closing.

One day, Bev pointed at a hulking passerby in the window. "That's Andy," she said. Across the street, the former Golden Gloves champion followed the sluggish procession toward the library.

Shortly after that, we watched Chrissy, a retired yoga instructor, do the same. Then Sam. Lucas. Brendan. Leza. Mandy. Skipp. Our most dedicated gym members. By the month's end, all but one member had walked out on The Lab's ancient weights and cardio machines. Nelson. We had helped him correct the posterior pelvic tilt and tight pectorals he'd developed as a result of riding a desk. Bev was in hospice when he left a voice mail canceling his membership. The next day, I saw him in the window heading toward the library.

I slipped on my sweatshirt and followed him. Nelson wore a trench coat and flip-flops. While I shadowed him I thought of everyone who had quit the gym recently. They reminded me of the movie *Invasion of the Body Snatchers* (the remake with Donald Sutherland—see, I'm not totally ignorant about horror), where extraterrestrials invade Earth by copying human life forms and killing the originals. Only an alien invasion could compel someone like Nelson to abandon the iron.

Looming in the sunlight, the library seemed like a pleasant place. The grounds sparkled, devoid of the rubbish I'd gotten used to seeing around large city branches. I tailed Nelson past hedges, birdbaths, a pair of stone lions. Inside, he turned left on a split staircase at the back of the entrance hall. I hung back, wondering what to do. Nelson didn't interest me. Playing pocket pool under the chandeliers, surrounded by empty check-out machines and abstract paintings, I realized not even the library interested me. The fact that Bev was wasting away in a hospital bed while the town sat on its butt in a book boneyard—that bothered me.

Still, I figured I might as well see what the big deal was about. Once you got past the check-out area, I had to admit you went on an excursion unlike anything you'd expect in a small-town public library. Floor-to-ceiling bookcases filled dozens of cavernous connecting rooms. Everything to know about cooking, Western history, archery, visual arts, military science, down to the narrowest treatments of the most obscure subsets of any scholarly interest you could imagine.

Amidst these impressive resources, little room remained for seating. People lined the walls or occupied odd nooks, squeezed into cubicle desks that took me back to my college days. No one sat side by side. They kept their distance to each other like men in a public urinal. My gut instinct told me to move toward these studious loners, get a peek at what consumed their attention. But I decided to be discreet and stuck to the inner aisles where I encountered no one.

Wandering among the stacks, I got the paranoid impression that the people here were not their normal selves—that they'd been drugged by something circulating in the air. The feeling clicked for me when I saw Nelson hunched over a laptop. They're waiting to die, I thought. Like my mom when her stomach slowly filled with fluid and we would watch TV together.

I hurried back to the gym. I stared at the brick building in the window and thought, *I'm never going back to that place again.*

But of course I did.

And that's when the really weird shit happened.

Her name was Barbee. Yes, two e's.

"Dear George John Wayne Kuato," her email read. "My name is Barbee Devereaux. I'm 22 years old. I want to be a fitness model. Unfortunately, I've been diagnosed with stage 4 lung adenocarcinoma. I'm doing everything I can to fight it. I will be going through aggressive chemotherapy for several months. My question to you is, can you write a program to help me build strength before I start treatments? My goal is to combat the muscle loss that is bound to happen. Thank you for your time. Barbee."

This was three weeks after my library visit. Bev had died by then.

God, I missed her. Even from her hospital bed she had been my anchor in all this misfortune. Without her, The Lab's equipment served only to remind me that the town had ruined a good thing. Because in the end, the library—whatever its strange power over the community—could not be blamed for the gym's demise. People made their choices. And if my mom was any example, they chose to escape. Into alcohol. Netflix. Even obscure intellectual pursuits. My best bet was to make my own escape and find people like Bev in some other town where I might make a living. In the meantime, I had started a website advertising my online coaching services.

And here was my first client, Barbee.

I did some research and emailed her a program. She responded with questions about volume and nutrition. Our conversations grew so involved we started Skyping.

A small voice in my head said, "You should refer these questions to her medical team." A loud voice in my head said, "She wants your help. She needs you. You can make a difference with her." Which voice do you think I listened to?

The loud voice spoke to the part of me that had helplessly watched my mom die. It sold Barbee to me like a commercial —"*For only a handful of ethically questionable decisions, you too, George John Wayne Kuato, can gain redemption!*" Of course, that was to make me look better in my own eyes. Because Barbee could pass for Bev in old pictures I had seen. With a hook like that, any objectivity I pretended to maintain in our online coaching relationship was bullshit.

And when the redemption story didn't hold up anymore, I made up a new story.

Sometimes it's not the message but the messenger who can turn around someone's fight against a life-threatening disease. In my revised Barbee story, the messenger was me. We were bound to cross a line sometimes.

We exchanged texts. Selfies. Spotify playlists. Soon I felt like I'd slipped inside a Barbee Devereaux hologram. I moved with her virtual projection through her day-to-day struggles. I felt aligned with her thoughts and emotions. Yet the connection heightened my need for proximity—I yearned to *be* with Barbee. What did she smell like? How would it feel to walk beside her?

She refused to meet me, though. "Too much," she said. "Too soon. Besides, a sick girl has to be mysterious."

Then one day she texted me: "I want you to Skype me from your town's library."

A small voice in my head said, "Don't do it."

A loud voice in my head said, "What the fuck are you waiting for?"

Which voice do you think I listened to?

I went back to the building on Bauman's Hill. I found a conference room in the basement and set up my laptop. I opened the Skype app. Barbee smiled when she saw the stacks in the window behind me. As usual, she showed herself exclusively from the chest up.

She wore a bandanna on her head to hide the hair loss. I wanted to ask how treatments were going, but I knew that would upset her. She had stopped discussing her health or even exercises with me. "You gave me what I wanted. Now we can move on to other things," she had told me in an email. She had fired me as her fitness coach and engaged me for more personal therapy.

"Satisfied?" I said softly. When it came to libraries I barely spoke above a whisper.

Barbee fired her words off like a drill instructor: "Show me your cock."

"You're kidding," I said, at normal volume.

But my inner voices were arguing.

"Please. I want to see it."

I checked the window for potential witnesses, then repositioned the laptop and unbuttoned my fly.

"Don't be a tease," Barbee said. "Keep it out there, George. Stroke it."

"Barbee, this is nuts."

"Your balls, too. I want to see them. Tickle them for me, like I would do if I could be there."

"Barbee, it's kind of busy here. I could get caught."

"Then be quick. We'll come together."

I gave it my best, but felt self-conscious.

"Could you at least scoot back a little?" I said.

"A sick girl has to be mysterious."

"But it feels stupid with just me—"

"Trust me, I'm in this, too. Come on, George. Hurry."

Barbee must have sensed my difficulties, because after a minute she said, "I've never seen a curved penis before. It makes me so horny."

"Oh, Barbee…"

"Shit, I'm almost there. Come with me!"

"God, you're so hot. Okay, I'm ready."

"I'll count it down. Ten… nine… eight…"

"*Ouch*!"

"What happened?"

"Got caught on my zipper. Keep going."

Barbee resumed the countdown. When she got to three, she switched to hand signs.

At zero, my gorgeous Skype partner clapped her hand to her mouth. At the same time, I shot my load like a man on weed and Viagra. I zipped carefully, then wiped the desktop with the hem of my shirt.

"Barbee, what the fuck."

She giggled. "It's like secretly masturbating in church without the guilt."

"You're amazing."

"Let's do it again."

I hadn't felt such vigor since my teenage years.

She was right—this was like secretly masturbating in church without the guilt. You felt you were being naughty, but not vile. We did it two more times.

The next day, I wore more sensible attire. A pair of old sweatpants to avoid zipper mishaps. A XXXL windbreaker for quick concealment.

The conference room became our daily rendezvous point.

What Barbee enjoyed most—perhaps because of the very

real threat to her life—was the degree of risk in our online sex games. Over the next few weeks, she pushed it as far as she could.

She said, "Jerk off in front of the window."

She said, "Show me your asshole."

She said, "Did you bring the zucchini?"

She said, "Eat it." Not referring to the zucchini.

Between our antics, I walked around the library.

The library seemed to have no end. Its four floors consisted entirely of lobbies and interconnecting rooms—vaults so vast a whole town could spread out in them. Occasionally in the aisles I came across some vagabond browser sitting on the floor with their back to me. Against my curious gut instinct, I steered clear of these gutter scholars as I avoided the cubicle desk people.

On rare occasions, I glimpsed one of the library's staffers. These hunchbacked old ladies pushed carts loaded with materials that needed shelving. An acrid odor followed them.

Funny, I thought, how this strange, depressing place now held something close to charm for me. Without the library, Barbee and I would lack the thrill of coming together as if everything depended on it.

"You give me a reason to live," she said. "Now smear that Chinese mustard on your cock."

I almost got caught once. I was pulling a dildo from my satchel when I heard the door open. I replaced the dildo and turned to see a young man of medium height staring at me from the threshold. He had an extended goatee and wore a T-shirt with a pterodactyl on it under a caption that said FAP FAP FAP. He held a tablet case. His bleary eyes said he might have seen the dildo.

"Oh, excuse me." He ducked out without closing the door.

The man's intrusion added to our excitement. George/Kuato the mutant conjoined twins couldn't hold an Arnold Schwarzenegger prayer candle to George John Wayne Kuato the library masturbator.

You would think I would run out of reserves. Instead, my stamina kept pace with Barbee's inspirations. After the goateed man walked in on me, she staged me in the most ridiculous positions she could imagine. The aphrodisiac of sheer panic sustained me through these wild, conspicuous milkings. "Stop looking back at the window," Barbee shouted while I humped a Barney hand puppet in a corner.

Like a drug addict, I lost sense of time acting out her increasingly quirky fantasies. Sometimes hours passed while I stared at my laptop between calls. Next thing I knew, the fluorescent lights would blink twice, telling patrons we had five minutes to conclude business. I would go home and collapse—I hardly ate by then—and wait for the sun to shine through my bedroom window. The library opened at 6 a.m. now that August had come.

When I slept, I dreamed of the dead. Once I dreamed I was with my mom watching TV. She spoke to me, but I turned up the volume to drown out her voice. Another time I dreamed Bev was inside The Lab banging on the window. She kept shouting something at me, but I couldn't hear her from across the street. I turned off Main Street and trekked uphill toward the library.

I thought about Barbee constantly. How she got off so violently she nearly fell out of her seat. How she giggled when she finished climaxing.

One day, after we'd failed to stay in sync, she promised that when I called her again she would fully reveal herself. Imagine my frustration when I returned from a break to find the goateed man at my desk.

"Oh, excuse me," he said.

I shut the door behind me and squeezed into a cubicle desk around the corner.

I decided to wait out the usurper. He would eventually take a break from his studies. Then he would come back and find me with a vegetable in my ass or screwing some sort of hand puppet.

I realize how irrational that sounds, but in my mind the conference room had become my sacred space. I would not call Barbee again until I took my rightful place before the altar.

Four seats away from me, an Asian man stood and stretched. I snuck a glance at him—he too had a goatee, only patchy and pubic-hairy, and looked like he hadn't slept in days. He wore a T-shirt with a bunch of red-fanged furballs on it that I recognized from my mom's favorite movie, *Critters* ("a cult classic," she used to say, not knowing it's a rip-off of an *Outer Limits* episode — again, I'm not totally pop-culture ignorant). Perhaps to repay me for encroaching on his space, the man edged down the narrow aisle toward me.

As he passed, he dropped a message on my desk: *"Meet me by the Small Press section in the Literature & History Room. We need to talk."* When I looked up again, he was gone.

In an odd way, his scribbled note excited me. From what I had seen, socializing didn't happen here. Something in the library's acrid, air-conditioned air isolated people even when we passed each other in the restroom or lobby. Being contacted by another patron in this fashion tapped into the same transgressive, life-affirming urge that drove me to hump hand puppets. But when I imagined meeting this man, I realized his cloak-and-dagger gesture had come too late. Other than my video chats, I had no resources for undercover business. I decided I should tell him so I wouldn't be distracted when I called Barbee.

I went to the second-floor meeting place. A librarian sorted materials on the small-press shelves. A pungent odor hung in the air, sharp as a recent skunk attack. What looked like a red wine stain darkened the beige carpet beneath the wheels of the old woman's book cart. No sign of my cult classic-loving secret agent. I hung back in a nearby section. When the librarian finally rolled her cart away, I still had not seen the man in the *Critters* T-shirt.

Too bad for him if he thought he could waste my time again, I thought. I went back to the conference room.

Pterodactyl Boy had left. Someone had cleaned the room recently. The tile floor had been mopped and the desk wiped down. The scent of cleaning agents mingled with the overpowering bouquet of Eau de Librarian. I wondered what these ladies ate that made them smell so potent.

I closed the door and set up my laptop. In my head, I told Pterodactyl Boy: Go ahead and come back. Try to claim the room again. Same goes for you too, Secret Asian Man. Breeze in at your convenience. But be warned. Barbee's going to make me pay dearly for what she's about to show me. I have a bag full of lube, dildos, pocket pussies, hand puppets, wigs, lingerie, vegetables and artisanal cheeses if you think I'm joking.

This next Skype call is going to break the Internet. Kim Kardashian can't hold a devotional candle to George John Wayne Kuato the library masturbator.

I fell into a sneezing fit that I blamed on the room's stink. Then I called Barbee.

"Hey, what's wrong?"

"I just talked to my doctor," she said. "The treatments aren't working."

"Oh, shit. What does that mean?"

"They're giving me six months."

"Oh, Barbee."

"Pull out your cock, George. Get it nice and hard. Make me feel better."

"Aren't there other options?"

"Show me your asshole."

"No, I mean for treatment."

"I'm going to ask for more chemo. Did you bring the cucumber and goat cheese?"

"Yeah. What about some sort of immunotherapy?"

"I'll ask for that, too. Stick the goat cheese in your ass and put the cucumber in your mouth."

"Wouldn't it be easier the other way around?"

"Don't question me, George. My day's been bad enough already. Just spoon some of the cheese with your finger and do what I tell you."

I took off my sweatpants and got in position. The room now reeked of ammonia, librarian B.O. and anal goat cheese.

"Now spread some cheese on the cucumber and take a bite."

I removed the cucumber from my mouth.

"Barbee, I know you don't like to talk about your health anymore, but you know, maybe if—"

"Not the cheese on the log, the butt cheese. Do it."

My inner voices argued, but there I was, half-naked, munching on a cucumber that tasted of my ass. Mixed with hints of lavender and wild fennel and the room's walloping odors. You can't blame me if I scrambled to find a happy place in my mind. Instead, I remembered my dream of Bev shouting through The Lab's front window. I heard the warning I'd blanked from memory:

"It's not what you think!"

Chunks of tainted cucumber fell from my mouth.

Like a cheap, cinematic dream-shimmer effect, my ravishing Barbee un-Barbeed on my laptop screen. In her place sat a monster with crimson eyes, ram-like horns and skin like a charred corpse.

"Oh no, that's not good enough," it said. It sounded like Bill Cosby speaking through wet gravel. "Do it again, George. Extra butt cheese this time."

I gaped. More cucumber left my lips.

"Don't you want to see my tight little pussy?"

I made a noise like a cat hocking up a hairball.

"Crap." The Un-Barbee monster addressed someone off-screen: "Cleanup in Conference Room C. Hurry." Then to me again: "So now you know."

I managed to croak, "What are you?"

"A demonically metastasized growth stemming from your town's repressed desires. A kind of supernatural, psychosexual malignancy."

"But what does that mean?"

"We consume people's life force through their sexual energy. Now my turn, Nancy Drew: How did you break our masturbation spell?"

"A loved one helped me in a dream."

It nodded. "There were two others like you. They hadn't figured everything out yet, but they were beginning to suspect."

Pterodactyl Boy and Secret Asian Man, I thought. Their subconscious dream messengers must have warned them they were under masturbation spells, too.

Before I could get my sweatpants back on, the door opened.

In walked another Un-Barbee with cat eye glasses and runs in its stockings. It laid its charcoal hand on my shoulder.

"A shame," it said. "You've got plenty of vigor left."

If these pages smell a little like ass and goat cheese, I apologize.

But when I opened the cheese log, I had not foreseen that a sexual demon would alter my chemical makeup with a smelly mystical potion, then turn me into paper and fold and bind me. I had not expected to become part of the library's enormous collection.

"Hmm, let's merge you with Muir," the first demon said, supervising from my laptop. "He's goofy in the same way you are."

This from a horned being that induced me to eat my semen for a girl with cancer.

At least the Un-Barbees commit to their archival pretense. Along with Mr. Muir, the Scottish-named Secret Asian Man and a wannabe sorcerer to judge by his occult fiction, the Un-Barbees have allowed me to tell my story.

I chose to record the truth. By contrast, the primary creative force sealed inside this book has chosen to tell lies. I may not be much of a fiction guy, but I actually mean "lies" in a positive sense. If you can get past the occasional crudeness in Mr. Muir's stories, you'll appreciate his gift for illuminating the sick and desperate aspects of the human condition. Although despite my lack of imagination, or maybe because of it, I suppose I've managed to do that too, sadly.

We were all so stupid, every library-going one of us. We let the Un-Barbees exploit our fantasies so they could devour our sexual energy. Even worse, we *created* these monsters. We sat around and let the hidden parts of our natures divide and expand into a malignant growth.

I want you to know something. If you're reading this, chances are the Un-Barbees have come to your town. This book was transferred to your local branch. You're reading it to kill time between wanking or diddling yourself. You're caught in a masturbation spell involving God knows what.

But you can still escape if you listen to me right now.

It's not what you think.

Do you hear me?

Whatever it is that feels so good right now, it's an illusion.

The deadliest sort.

Listen:

Fap fap fap

Don't touch yourself so much.

Don't believe everything you see.

Don't even believe me.

Put down this book.

Get off your ass.

Do this for me. For Pterodactyl Boy. For Mr. Muir. For everyone you hold dear.

Step into the daylight.

Throw a sucker punch at mortality.

Do something amazing.

Love for your life.

THE HADDONFIELD HIT SQUAD

As with every story worth telling, this one begins with a dream that I was banging Charlize Theron. Not Theron as one of her movie characters, but as her self-parody reenacting the viral YouTube video "Sittin' on tha Toilet" in an old *Funny or Die* episode I had watched the night before.

The Oscar-winning actress was giving it to me cowgirl-style, mean mugging me and saying "sittin' on tha toilet" over and over, when an invisible hand squeezed my shoulder. "Charles," a disembodied voice said. "Charles," the voice repeated while I squeezed Charlize Theron's breasts and pretended my name was not Charles.

"Charles." I opened my eyes and saw my wife hovering over me. She wore her brown faux leather jacket and smelled of herbal ointments. "I'll be back around six. Let Iggy out to pee, okay?" She kissed me on the cheek and headed off to massage people, something my wussy writer's hands could never do.

I climbed out of bed, dressed and let the dog out. I watched Iggy pee on the garden art my wife had made from my old powerlifting trophies without asking if she could repurpose them. That damn woman, I thought. Even more than my mom, she had a talent for interrupting my sex dreams. Not the ones I wished she would, like the dream where I made out with Steve, my high-school football buddy, but the rare awesome dreams with celebrities like Charlize Theron.

Kara's into witchy stuff—tarot readings, smudging ceremonies, crystals and gemstones, that sort of thing—so maybe she had trained herself to monitor my dream activity for kicks. She can practically read my mind, anyway—we've been together for twenty-nine years.

I herded Iggy inside and penned him in the kitchen with me. Now that my latest collection was in my publisher's hands, I didn't know what to do with my spare time. An inner voice suggested I watch the original *Halloween* in preparation for the upcoming sequel reuniting Laurie Strode with Michael Myers. I didn't want to look for the DVD though, so I decided against it. I poured a cup of coffee instead and pulled up Facebook on my laptop.

A friend's kid was going to star in an off-Broadway musical. Another friend had found out their cat had cancer. Another friend had been mansplained to. The usual stuff. I scrolled through my news feed, past kid pics, pet pics, writers drinking beer together pics, selfies, puppy videos, until I came upon a picture that my friend Shane had posted.

He had found a teaser for the much anticipated *Halloween* sequel. The image showed Michael Myers's hand holding his trademark butcher knife.

The problem was the sharp edge faced out, according to Shane. This led to an argument in the comments about the proper way for Myers to hold a knife. The hand-to-hand combat experts agreed that he should hold it with the sharp edge out for an offensive attack. My friend Shane replied, "Since when did Myers go for Navy SEAL training? Which movie was that?" That got me picturing Michael Myers as an action hero... like my dad's favorite fictional super spy, Mack Bolan.

Mack Myers. Ha. It was just dumb enough to be a short story. I didn't feel like writing it, though. Instead, I posted a joke about it on Facebook and waited for the "likes" to come in. By waiting, I mean I ate scrambled eggs, watched a Lillian Chong video on SploogeTube and went back to bed.

Maybe there was something in those Kroger large brown eggs. A psychoactive hormone or something. Whatever the case, I fell asleep and had a dream even more vivid than Charlize Theron bouncing on my dick and shouting "sittin' on tha toilet" over and over. In this life-like dream, I was cruising in a station wagon down a tree-lined street. My hands looked extra big on the steering wheel and my head felt heavy and hot. I touched my cheek and realized I had a mask on my face.

My left middle finger pushed the signal lever down. Turning, I saw a bald man talking with a sheriff on the sidewalk across the street. I did a double take and almost ran into a parked van.

"Watch out!" A voice said.

I looked down. Through my mask's eye holes, I made out a baby man with shoe-polish black hair sticking through a hole in my jumpsuit. Because of my extra long arms, he had room to rest his tiny hands on the bottom of the steering wheel. He wore infant-sized, fingerless motorcycle gloves.

"Pull up over here," the baby man said. You'll have to imagine his Austrian accent. If I write it out H.P. Lovecraft-style, it will ruin the flow of the story. "Now. Come on. Do it."

I signaled a right turn, but kept staring at my conjoined twin. Holy shitballs, how cool is this, I thought. I had a Kuato attached to my stomach like the mutant in *Total Recall*—only Arnold Schwarzenegger himself was Kuato and he was bossing me around like Master the dwarf in another science fiction film I liked but not as much as *Total Recall*, *Mad Max Beyond Thunderdome*.

"Come on, we're here," Kuatonegger shouted, pounding his little fists on the steering wheel. "Turn right. What are you waiting for?"

At the last instant, I swerved into the parking lot of a brick building with a red-on-white sign that said TRAMER'S TITIL-LATIONS. Only someone had covered the ITILLATION with black spray paint. Very funny.

I parked the station wagon between a Pontiac Firebird and another station wagon. A man walked out of the store carrying a black plastic bag.

"A porn shop?" A gravelly voice said behind me. I looked in the rearview mirror. My heart thudded against my rib cage — holy shitballs, I thought again, I was staring into the beady eyes of Freddy Krueger. Freddy. Fucking. Krueger.

The man deserves that many periods. He scared me that bad when the first *Nightmare on Elm Street* came out.

He didn't seem as scary though, he became more iconic the older I got. His red-and-green sweater and brown fedora attracted too much attention, in my opinion, compared to Michael Myers's and Jason Vorhees's generic jumpsuits. Still, the fanboy in me broke a sweat thinking how I was cruising around Myers's hometown, Haddonfield, with an Arnold Schwarzenegger baby man and Freddy Fucking Krueger.

And yes, I realized where I fit into this picture, but I was saving confirmation for a mirror where I could really see myself, not just my William Shatner forehead in the rearview.

Freddy Krueger hooked his dirty finger knives over the top of the passenger seat, which had been empty for no reason except that maybe he looked scarier meeting my eyes in the rearview mirror. "A porn shop," he repeated. "I can't believe we're going to hit someone in a goddamn porn shop."

"The Haddonfield Hit Squad goes where the money is," Kuatonegger said. "And here is where the money is, Freddy. Get your ass to the porn shop!"

I might have been laughing at the *Total Recall* reference, or maybe I was breathing harder from the thrill of realizing we were assassins. Whichever it was, I was distracted enough to bump my noggin on the door pillar when I climbed out of the station wagon. The real Michael Myers is at least six inches taller than me.

And when I say "real" Michael Myers, I mean the intellectual property of whoever owns the *Halloween* franchise. Which brings me to a point I have to address before going forward. This portion of the story is not about Kuato, Michael Myers, Freddy Krueger, Sam Loomis, Laurie Strode, Laurie Strode's dad, Annie Brackett, Bennett Tramer, Paul Freedman or any other cinematic characters it references (i.e., Lynda Van der Klok, sorry to parenthesize you—you get a whole scene, though). This is not an attempt to exploit a franchise and it is definitely not a fan fiction piece. I'm telling you about a dream I had. I want you to know about it because it was very realistic and because it began with a different dream of me banging Charlize Theron. Almost every story worth telling begins with me fictitiously banging Charlize Theron.

In fact, let's be clear that I dreamed I was *Mack* Myers, not Michael Myers. And my teammate Freddy was not a demonic serial killer but an expert in dream wet work who went by the code name "Kill Zone." Sure, I made that up just now. But Freddy should have an action name, too.

So now that I've covered my authorial ass, let's return to the porn store parking lot where Kill Zone and I listened to Kuatonegger give us our first assignment.

"Our job is tee-yurmination," he said. "We are to kill da son of da proprietah who owns dis shop." Whoops—see, I told you it wouldn't be good if I tried to write his Austrian accent.

"Who's the target?" Kill Zone said.

"Bennett Tramer," Kuatonegger said. "His father is paying good money for this."

Now there's a back story probably not mentioned on the Halloween Series Wiki, I thought. Thinking was all I could do in my hulking dream body. That and small gestures that didn't interfere with foreordained dream business.

What was more, I realized Laurie Strode would be sad to learn we had killed a boy she liked. But oh, well. We were the Haddonfield Hit Squad and had people to see and one-liners to drop while we stabbed and slashed them to death. We headed toward the porn store entrance.

"What are you doing?" Kuatonegger struck my sternum with a backward headbutt. "You forgot the chopper. Get to the chopper!"

"He means the knife," Kill Zone said.

Now, how could I have forgotten that? So Kuatonegger could work in Arnold's best-known quote from *Predator*? Of course.

I unlocked the back door on my side and searched for my signature murder weapon. I found it under a bag of Chili Cheese Fritos that Kill Zone had opened with his finger knives. My fifteen-inch stainless steel blade was more stabber than chopper the way I used it, I wanted to say, but only managed more loud breathing.

"One, two, the Haddonfield Hit Squad is coming for you," Kill Zone said, wiggling his Frito-stained finger knives. He seemed to dig the name as much as I did.

We entered Tramer's Tits. The adult video emporium smelled of lube and new carpet. *The Gilmore Girls* played on a flat screen TV behind the front counter. This dream was not just vivid, it was filled with anachronisms... not that I caught them all in my Mack Myers mindset.

Bennett Tramer turned from the TV to face us. I can't remember what the actual character looked like because I've only seen *Halloween 2* twice. The young man with a stack of DVDs in his hands had a handsome Shaun Cassidy face, though.

Kill Zone scraped his finger knives across the pillar next to the counter. "Da doo ron *RUN*," he said. Tramer blinked, not getting Kill Zone's incongruous reference. Tramer's 1970s teen-idol look-alike had covered The Crystals' hit song "Da Doo Ron Ron" on his first solo album, *Shaun Cassidy*. Sadly for Tramer, he would not have time to research Cassidy's discography.

"What can I help you guys with?" the young man said.

Kuatonegger pointed at him. "Come on, Bennett. Let's party."

It was beautiful. Arnold had originally said that to another Bennett in his best one-liner movie ever, *Commando*. Even in Mack Myers mode, some part of me must have appreciated my mutant twin's bon mot, because instead of doing my stabbing thing I just stood there breathing loudly.

"What are you doing, kill him," Kuatonegger said, kicking at me like Iggy when he wants to spread out on the couch.

Reaching across the counter with my extra core strength, I grabbed Tramer by the neck and lifted him off his feet. I drove my knife into his chest, then tossed him at Lorelai Gilmore singing "I Will Always Love You" on the flat screen TV. While I still held the knife up, I checked it like the young Michael Myers does in the first *Halloween* to make sure the sharp edge of the blade faced in. Come to think of it, maybe that's why he looks at his knife before killing Big Sister—to make sure the sharp edge faced in. For God's sake, he's Michael Myers, he doesn't need proper knife-fighting skills.

While I wiped my knife with a paper towel, Kill Zone grabbed one of the DVDs Tramer had dropped when I stabbed him. *Monsters of Jizz, Volume 9*. Laughing all the way, he read the back of the DVD case while I drove to our next assignment.

Um, I'm going to skip how we killed dumbass Paul Freedman. Annie Brackett's boyfriend went out messily thanks to Kill Zone. Suffice it to say "Old Jerko" would never throw eggs or soap windows again.

Now we get to the gnarliest part of my story.

For our third job, we pulled up to Laurie Strode's dad's office. Like I said, I don't remember *Halloween* frame by frame (I know people who do, though) so I'm not even sure the place appears in it. It's not a detail I would bother to Google. Anyway, instead of a building with a sign advertising STRODE REALTY we parked in front of my friend Jay's house. It was as good a site as any for a dream that has nothing to do with the real estate business.

Reluctantly, I turned off the 8-track player. We were halfway through Shaun Cassidy's cover of "That's Rock 'n' Roll," a song that had been written by Eric Carmen. It became the second of three consecutive top 10 hits for Cassidy... pretty good for a debut solo album.

Under cover of night now, we snuck around the side of my friend's house. Hiding behind a bush like the real Michael Myers stalking Laurie Strode and her friends, we came upon a black dog peeing on a tree. I reached for the stray, but a vague fondness for its kind overpowered my murderous instincts.

This was one of the few events in the dream I managed to change, by the way. Even Kuatonegger agreed with my animals-over-people compassion. "Hasta la vista, baby," he said as the pooch trotted off.

Using my extra leg strength, I kicked in a side door and led us through Jay's kitchen into the dining room. On the way, I caught my reflection in the hallway mirror. Fuck yeah, I thought. You could have used me in Universal Studios' Halloween Horror Nights with Kuatonegger and his cyborg eye as a bonus thrill... anyone who would wait two hours in line for a haunted house tour would love us. Not that I thought that far ahead, but I knew we looked good—or evil, to be more precise.

Laurie's blonde friend didn't seem impressed, however. "You guys totally can't be here." Lynda Van der Klok stood from the dining room table and marched toward us. She was topless because this is a *Halloween* dream and even that movie showed female breasts.

Van der Klok looked at Kill Zone's non-weaponized hand. "Wait, is that... *Monsters of Jizz, Volume 9?*"

Kill Zone was too busy staring at her breasts to hear her.

We might have stood there a while, but I felt some serious mojo after catching my reflection in the mirror. I took Van der Klok to the floor and made my chopper go *STAB! STAB! STAB!* on her.

"This is totally unfair," she screamed, while I worked faster than Bishop demonstrating his knife trick in *Aliens*, not an Arnold Schwarzenegger or John Carpenter movie but at least horror-ish so not *totally* inappropriate here. "I'm just the file clerk at Strode Realty."

Kuatonegger consigned her to Valhalla with a one-liner he made up himself: "Consider yourself foreclosed."

Not to be left out, Kill Zone wiggled his finger knives and said, "I'm your boyfriend now, Lynda."

"That was kind of lame, Freddy," Kuatonegger said. Remember, I made up the code name "Kill Zone" a few pages ago to distinguish our dream-proficient wet boy from the real Freddy Krueger. In case you're not keeping track.

"Totally," Lynda Van der Klok said, and died.

Kuatonegger and I covered in blood, and Kill Zone still

clutching his *Monsters of Jizz, Volume 9* DVD, we crept upstairs to the second floor. I hoped I wouldn't run into my friend Jay. I didn't want to have to stab him in the middle of another confession that he loves Stevie Nicks. I mean, I love Stevie Nicks, too —her music gets lots of play in our house, considering my wife practices witchcraft—but when my friend gets drunk he tells me how much he loves Stevie Nicks, and I didn't know if I could overpower my Mack Myers urge to kill human beings, including fans of Stevie Nicks.

Down the hall, the man I'd seen talking with a sheriff emerged from a bedroom. Behind Dr. Samuel Loomis was our target—Laurie Strode. Loomis wore his signature trench coat, Strode a button-down shirt and jeans similar to what she wore in the first movie's climax.

The heroine looked us over. "Wait, is that… *Monsters of Jizz, Volume 9?*" she said.

To be clear, like Lynda Van der Klok, Strode didn't seem aroused by Kill Zone's stolen video so much as baffled by its inclusion in a tableau involving supernaturally powerful executioners and a tiny mutant cyborg.

Loomis pulled his Smith & Wesson on us. "Back off, gentlemen, or it's your funeral."

"You mean funerals," Kill Zone said.

"Whatever, you're a fucking choirboy compared to us, Loomis, a choirboy!" Kuatonegger said. Then, topping off *End of Days* with the *Commando* line he'd used at the porn store, he added: "Let's party."

And God help us, we did party. But not with the stabbing and slashing and one-liners you would expect by now.

Oh, no. I didn't march toward our combatants like an automaton with the knife raised (sharp edge in). Instead, I put down the chopper and pulled down Kuatonegger's trousers. With my extra long fingers, I stroked the mutant's chubby Kuatoweenie. Its smoothness triggered vague, soothing memories that I later understood to be moments when I had accidentally touched Iggy's furry little pug penis.

And I do mean accidentally. Don't believe my wife when she

says I touch our dog's dick on purpose. I only did that with Kuatonegger.

He fought me, at first. He hit me with all the bony parts he could and *gyaaaaaahhed* like an Arnold scream compilation video. But then he accepted my tender if rapey reach-around and even guided me with his fingerless motorcycle-gloved hand. If you can't beat Mack Myers, you might as well let him beat you.

"Do it doucement," he said, which Arnold doesn't say in *True Lies* but it's still in an Arnold movie. "Do it... very slowly." He sounded almost French for a moment.

Not to be left out, Kill Zone came up behind me and traced his blades along my backside. "I'm your boyfriend now, Mack," he said. Inside, I shuddered. Nothing against Kill Zone, but he had taken an excessive interest in the *Monsters of Jizz, Volume 9* DVD. Given he had fish knives for fingers, I didn't want to explore my sexuality with him too deeply.

It was getting awfully hot inside my mask.

Loomis said, "Yikes. Come on, Laurie. Let's get out of here."

They walked past us, down the stairs and out the front door.

Meanwhile, the Haddonfield Hit Squad got deep into a different kind of action. Kill Zone stopped trying to kiss me, what with his hat brim and my mask and conjoined mutant twin in the way, and bent down to watch me pleasure Kuatonegger.

"Jesus," he said, squinting at the nub in my fingers. "Is that a pecker or a tumor?"

"Shut up, it's not a tumor," Kuatonegger cried. He unleashed his own jizz monster in Kill Zone's burned-up face.

At this point, I wondered.

How had this happened? How had we turned from slasher villains into slash fiction characters?

You'll recall me wondering about Bennett Tramer's back story on the *Halloween Series Wiki*. Pretty meta for a dream thought, right? So was my suspicion now that events had strayed from their intended course. We were way out of character. I mean, there's no reason the three of us couldn't be gay, given we had no official back story to say otherwise, but our homoerotic frenzy felt forced, tacked on like the end of a

Cloverfield movie where the writer goes, "Oh yeah, we're supposed to have a giant creature in this story and it's got to be gay."

Someone laughed.

I looked up. Laurie Strode was back, floating near the ceiling. Or should I say, a dream-puppet simulation of Laurie Strode floated near the ceiling. Damn. I now had no doubt who had meddled in our slashing business... I recognized that self-satisfied snicker mocking the homoeroticized Haddonfield Hit Squad in Jamie Lee Curtis's voice.

Speaking of voices, I found mine. "You really can get into my dreams," I said.

"Duh. I've only been sleeping next to you every night for like a thousand years."

Kill Zone cackled. He had no idea what we were talking about. "Come to Freddy," he said, and charged at my wife in Laurie Strode disguise. Mind you, he had Frito dust on his finger knives and mutant jizz on his face.

Perhaps as an inside joke about her witchiness, Kara wrinkled her Strode nose like Samantha from *Bewitched*. Kill Zone froze.

And when he turned to face us, he wasn't Freddy "Kill Zone" Krueger anymore. He was my football buddy Steve from high school.

To be clear, I never kissed Steve... I don't know why I dreamed I made out with him. I certainly never fantasized about it. I may have swatted his butt during football practice a time or two, but I never fantasized about kissing him on the mouth. Let me repeat: I never fantasized about kissing Steve, all right? And I didn't want to kiss him now.

For one thing, brotherly reach-arounds aside, I'm not gay—not that there's anything wrong with being gay—for another, Steve looked exactly as he had thirty years ago, which placed him below the age of consent in some states. As if he gave a crap. Still holding the *Monsters of Jizz, Volume 9* DVD, he thumbed open his fly and pulled out his underage prick. He flashed me bedroom eyes.

"I should never have told you about that dream," I told my Laurie Strode-spouse floating near the ceiling.

She smiled. "But you did."

"Seriously, why are you so into this man-love thing?"

"Man-love isn't a 'thing,' Charles, it's beauty in motion."

"You're a weirdo."

"A weirdo who's getting you beer on the way home."

"No beer is worth this," I said.

"Isn't it?"

"Please. Don't do this. Wake me up."

"Can't, I have a client coming in. Sweet dreams." She blew me a kiss. Then with an overdone Margaret Hamilton laugh, my witchy wife the dream-spoiler vanished.

Unfortunately for Kill Zone and Kuatonegger, the dream continues for at least another 50 paragraphs (I lost count) after this. I did the unthinkable next—I unmasked.

I couldn't stop myself. Even while massaging someone, Kara controlled the dream. She made me lay the white latex mask that gave me such a fearsome aspect on the carpet runner next to the chopper. Then she made me fall to my knees. Grinning idiotically, my buddy Steve moved toward me.

My God, I thought. He's like Bennett Tramer. He looks like Shaun Cassidy. Shorter hair, bigger muscles, wearing a varsity jacket instead of a sweater draped over a button-down shirt... but otherwise very Cassidy-like. I'm talking 1977 *Born Late* Shaun Cassidy... the man at his foxiest, *Tiger Beat* cover boy best. How had I never noticed this before?

As if he sensed his formidable charisma, Steve howled in ecstasy. "It's first and ten, baby. As in ten inches. Let's do this. On three!"

Thanks to my wife, I felt an overwhelming urge to perform fellatio on my gorgeous jock friend. I took a deep breath.

"Three, two, one—"

I placed my extra big hands on Steve's extra firm butt cheeks.

"—break!"

And took his extra long dick in my mouth.

"Do it doucement," Kuatonegger said. "Do it... very slowly."

I obeyed. But after a while, something felt off. You would think this was a delayed general reaction to my wife's abuse of slash fiction tropes, but no.

I missed my mask.

The feeling of latex enshrouding my face. The thrill of peeping at the world through a pair of eye holes. The freedom to project the darkness that everyone fears… the absence of empathy, the impersonality of the universe, whatever. *Evil*. That's what bothered me as I worked my French oral skills on Steve: I didn't feel evil anymore.

Suddenly, the presence of man meat in my mouth made me sick. Not because it tasted unpleasant or triggered some lousy ego complex, but because it aroused feelings intensely associated with love.

Damn it, I wasn't a lover. I was a stone cold killer. I pushed my old football buddy away from me. I grabbed my mask from the floor and put it on.

Booya. Just like that, I broke my wife's control over the dream. While an unseen piano played the opening notes of the *Halloween* theme, I got to my feet. Steve gawked at me.

"But it's first and ten —"

"Oh, knock it off," I said. "Kill Zone, are you in there? Come on, wake up." Ironic I should tell *him* that, I know.

Some of Kill Zone's old grimace crept back into Steve's face. "Help me, Mack. I don't want to be your boyfriend. Why did I say those things?"

"Because my wife hijacked my dream," I said. I nodded at his flagging erection. "Put that hog away."

"Oh, yeah. Sorry. Jesus, Mack. This is… well, it's a nightmare!"

"Goddamn right it is. And we're pulling out of it right now."

"How?"

I bent down and picked up the chopper.

"Look, guys," I said. "We are the Haddonfield Hit Squad. We are *professionals*. We have people to see and one-liners to drop while we stab and slash them to death. We just happened to have run into a minor setback. Sometimes it's unavoidable —"

"It's not a tumor," Kuatonegger said, glumly.

"We know, big guy. Snap out of it."

"Fuck you, asshole."

"That's better. Anyway, so we got caught with our pants down—literally. Now we're trapped in a dream of my wife's making. I've broken her spell, but I think it's best to escape this place in case she takes over again. I say we take out a new target, one that will force me to wake up. Then I can go back to sleep and start a new dream, one that *we* control."

Kill Zone said, "Sounds good. So who's the target?"

I raised the knife and drew a circle in the air with it. "Us."

"But the riddle of steel," Kuatonegger objected, philosophizing from one of Arnold's earliest movies, *Conan the Barbarian*. "If you kill us here, you'll die in the flesh."

"That's an urban legend, big guy. And *Urban Legend* is a completely different movie. Just think of it this way: When it comes to being mortally wounded, we've got the genes of Olympic athletes. Michael Myers has been shot dozens of times. He's also been beaten with a metal pipe and decapitated and electrocuted. And Freddy Krueger has also been decapitated, set on fire and sent to Hell several times. He even got blown up with a pipe bomb. And Arnold, he only died once on screen as far as I know… pretty good for a career spanning over three decades, right? What I'm saying is, we're based on characters who have a way of coming back from every conceivable manner of death. We'll come back from this, guys. What do you say—suicide pact?"

Kill Zone yawned. "I wished you'd killed me halfway through that long-ass speech. But yeah, suicide pact."

"Big guy?"

"Looks like we've been targeted for termination."

"Excellent."

Without further ado, I made my chopper go *STAB! STAB! STAB!* on my tiny mutant cyborg twin. "I'll be back," he said (going out on the best-known Arnold quote ever), and died.

"You bet you will."

I turned to Kill Zone next. Despite reclaiming the dream, I

still tingled from the magnetism of his virile Steve body—proof that Kara still exerted some influence on us, to my way of thinking. To ward off his good looks, I closed my eyes.

"Wait," I heard Kill Zone say.

"Don't back out now."

"I'm not. I just want to say… thanks, Mack. For being my friend. Hell, for being my boyfriend, even. I'll see you in the sequel, right?"

"*All* the sequels."

"And the reboots?"

"Even the reboots."

I made my chopper go *STAB! STAB! STAB!* on Kill Zone. When his corpse hit the carpet runner, he had transformed back into his fedora-rocking, Swiss cheese-faced self.

Finally, I made the chopper go *STAB! STAB! STAB!* on my chest. I fell to my knees and watched my blood run onto the carpet runner. *Hasta la vista, baby*, I thought.

But a minute later, my reflexes took over and I walked out of the house unscathed. As if in a trance, I got in the station wagon, cranked up Shaun Cassidy's *That's Rock'n'Roll Live* album on the 8-track player and cruised around my hometown.

Over the next few hours, I stabbed everyone in Haddonfield. My victims included Sam Loomis, Laurie Strode, Laurie Strode's dad and Annie Brackett, plus the people I'd stabbed earlier— including Lynda Van der Klok, who totally stayed dead while my friend Jay interrupted me to confess his love of Stevie Nicks and got himself stabbed in the process.

After I killed the last resident—the neighbor who wouldn't open the door for Laurie Strode when Michael Myers chased her in the first *Halloween*—I stabbed myself again to test an idea. Confirming my suspicion, I survived.

Why, I wondered. Because I couldn't die in my dream? How could that be? People died all the time in dreams and woke up with no harm done. It had to be something more. Then I thought of all the kills I'd racked up in the time it takes to watch a John Carpenter movie… some abominably evil shit. I mean, only a really evil bastard could butcher his comrades and slay a whole town in a robotic murder spree, right?

Which meant I was really evil—even eviler than Kill Zone and Kuatonegger. Perhaps *too* evil for my fellow hit men. Come to think of it, maybe they didn't deserve a spot in the sequels and reboots I had promised them. After all, some atom of humanity had made them too weak to defy the knife as I had done. Clearly, I faced some tough decisions moving forward.

Good thing I was a really evil bastard, or I would have lacked the nerve to break up the band and become the solo-slashing, wholeheartedly evil protagonist who is hijacking this narrative now and giving it the alternate title "Mack Myers Stabs the Whole World to Death," so much punchier than the vanilla "The Haddonfield Hit Squad."

But before I conclude, I'd like to take the opportunity here to declare I am the evilest rampaging son-of-a-bitch slasher-assassin who ever lived (my annoying double, Charles Austin Muir, makes it possible for me to exist in the outside world). My elemental evilness guarantees I can never be killed. Trust me, in every dream of me since the one the witch hijacked, I've tested my hypothesis that evil in a white latex mask never dies. In *Haddonfield Hit Squad 2, 4* (*3* had nothing to do with me), *5,6, H20, Resurrection* and even the Rob Zombie dream reboot, I've stabbed, shot, clubbed, suicide-bombed, decapitated myself and so on… and each time I've escaped to slash another day. Don't hate me—I can't help who I am: The carjacking, jumpsuit-wearing, asthmatic-sounding, coat hanger-hating personification of evil itself.

What's more, now that I've embraced my evilness I can travel like Kill Zone into other people's dreams. That includes Rob Zombie's dreams and yours. That's right. Because you rudely fell asleep a moment ago while reading "Mack Myers Stabs the Whole World to Death," I'm creeping up on you wearing a white sheet and Bob Simms's (Lynda Van der Klok's boyfriend) glasses. Do you hear that scary horror-movie breathing over your shoulder?

Yep, that's me, raising my chopper to go *STAB! STAB! STAB!* on you.

That's how Mack Myers ghosts you in your sleep (you really can die in real life if you die in your dream—I lied about that being an urban legend earlier, *HA!*).

That's rock'n'roll.

NOTES ON A COSMIC HORRORCORE ALBUM

Yeah, and you don't stop,
Cause it's 1-8-7 on a motherfucking flock

—YouTuber's remix of "Deep Cover" by Dr. Dre in reference to
Tragedy House

Congratulations. You have purchased a unique product. This limited edition cassette contains the final, previously unreleased recording of hip-hop artist Charles Austin Muir, who went by the name *C-Dex* (*Brown Boyz, 1998, Bored with Supremacy, 2006*). As far as I know, C-Dex was the only rapper to devote the last phase of his career to the works of horror author Thomas Ligotti.

As his occasional co-producer and close friend, I warned Muir his aesthetic turnabout would alienate his already narrow fan base. The by then middle-aged writer/rapper just looked at me and shrugged. He claimed he had quit worrying about the cruder points of the rap game since he had discovered Ligotti. He had seen the error of what he called his "lyrical quiescence" and determined to redeem himself in an album that projected the author's sense of the uncanny.

In a state of "mad atonement," as he put it, borrowing a phrase from his literary idol, Muir completed *Songs of a Dead Homey* in his basement studio in three weeks, fueled by coffee, whiskey and tuna fish sandwiches. He then mailed me a flash drive containing the tracks "to publish or consign to oblivion" as I pleased. By the time I received the package, he was on a plane bound for Jackson, Wyoming. From there he joined up with the Sect of Caligari.

Before I get to that, a few words about the songs you're about to hear. My favorites are "What's My Nameless" and "Dr. Loced Out's Asylum." I'm also fond of "Ambitionz az a Clown Puppet." Now, I know what you're thinking. You might look at the track list for this album and wonder if C-Dex aspired to be horrorcore's "Weird Al" Yankovic. The truth is he despised parody. As wholeheartedly as he had rapped about love and childhood, he threw himself into expressing Ligotti's subtly crafted visions of gnostic dread in a subgenre of hip-hop music that gravitates toward extreme violence and absurdism.

As for production value, let's just say my friend prized sensibility over sonics. Time and again I urged him to collaborate with a solid beatmaker if not me (we clashed repeatedly over the sampling in *Bored with Supremacy*), or at least study certain producers whose work I recommended. But Muir was ever an individualist when it came to solo projects. Generally speaking, he refused to consider influences he hadn't already discovered on his own.

Which brings me to the Sect of Caligari.

In case you didn't follow the news stories, the cult came about when a man by the user name of MCaligari187 began posting on the Thomas Ligotti Online forums (TLO is both a site dedicated to Ligotti and an online community). His bombastic writings attracted a small following. In an unethical use of the site, the popular MCaligari187 used chats and private messages to clandestinely recruit members for a commune he planned to establish in a mountainous region of Wyoming. My friend—known on the forums as CharlesDexterMuird—became one of the last to join his flock.

Of the cult, little is known. It consisted of over a hundred artists and thinkers who saw MCaligari187's writings as radical revisions of Ligotti. Its leader, however, conducted himself more like a horrorcore psychopath than a Ligottian renegade. On the night of Sept. 19, 2010, "Master Caligari," as he called himself, implemented a solution to the problem of human suffering no philosophical pessimist in their right mind would endorse.

Fortunately for historians, Muir managed to get audio for the event with his cell phone. Perhaps he had hoped to use excerpts in an art project. We will never know. Nor will we know if Master Caligari, born Jerusalem Michael Jones in 1978, used "187" (in his TLO user name) in the street sense, as a reference to murder. All we can be sure of is that Jones was diabolical, much like another Jones who died the year he was born.

The transcript that follows was originally re-posted by Muir's family on Thomas Ligotti Online on Jan. 16, 2013. For reasons they never explained to me, they altered the police transcriber's format and set off the sections with poetic subheadings. Minus the subheadings, I have republished the transcript in this booklet as a supplement to the famous cell-phone recording of Master Caligari's last address to his flock. Macabre as it may seem, I decided to include the recording as a bonus track along with an incomplete song, "Mo Manikins Mo Problems." I have the family's permission to do this, and I feel C-Dex would at least not disapprove.

So without further ado, I present *Songs of a Dead Homey*. I'm sorry I took seven years to release this, my friend. But you see your work is not yet ready for oblivion.

James "The Professor" Butler
B-Jam Records
Jan. 14, 2018

TRANSCRIPT

MASTER CALIGARI (MC): Good evening, children; sons and

daughters of abomination. As descendants of Adam, it is our curse to share in the pain of expulsion. We of the Tragedy House (*Note: MC seems to use this name interchangeably for both the assembly hall and the commune in a heroic sense*) suffer twice, for we are excluded from our own kind, who are outcasts of nature, driven from the kingdom of beasts. Let us thank the Great Pessimist (*Note: Probably a reference to Peter Wessel Zapffe, a Norwegian metaphysician who influenced Ligotti*), who taught that man can never return to the kingdom of beasts.

Now let us hold in our minds what unites us at this moment.

Madness, children. The madness of our convictions. The madness of renouncing the age-old ways. In these barren mountains, under blind stars, we live as misfits scornful of all privileges claimed by the mightiest of nature's predators, penning our farcical plays and dreaming up new pantomimes from our trunk full of costumes. Our cousins in the valley think us mad; let them lap up their spoils, the greediest of earth's consumers. Meanwhile, we smile through our makeup into the panic that sweeps humanity in the jaws of madness.

Tonight, I speak of madness: For who does not think of madness at the mention of Caligari?

Who among you does not recall the ending of that wicked little film (*Note: The Cabinet of Dr. Caligari, considered the quintessential work of German Expressionist cinema*), wherein the entire preceding story is revealed to be the fantasy of Francis, an inmate of an insane asylum? There is a reason I ask you to study the movie. That is to question its reliability, for in my mind Francis's narrative is not alone in warranting suspicion—we must give context to the second story that debunks the first. Compelled to soften Francis's tale of a hypnotist's murderous obsession and a sleepwalker programmed to kill, the filmmakers were obliged to recast it as a fabrication of mental illness, and yet in their invention we see the ultimate delusion.

For these men bowed to the overarching impulse to repress the truth that human beings exist as martyrs on the altar of a purposeless universe. Like courtiers in a Jacobean tragedy, we bleed for the sake of bleeding, powerless to break the cycle of causality and addicted to any haven from our terror of the slaughter. Even our little colony knows the urge to repress this sickening knowledge, for our isolation speaks to the instinct of all threatened creatures to seek higher ground.

As artists attuned to the human cry against a universe that is meaningless and unjust, we, children, are particularly sensitive; yet through our creativity and fellowship we have diminished the power of repression in order to sink deeper, with compassion and curiosity, into the cosmic panic, the underlying fears that torment us.

Indeed, as the Great Pessimist has shown, human beings dread not only death, but life itself. Not only the traumas and shocks, but the endless repetitions, the futile efforts. The mundane world leaves us incurably sick. We were doomed from the moment Adam ate from the Tree of Knowledge. Always, we feel the pangs of alarm as if we had swallowed poison and wait for its effect: In our imaginations, in that excess of cognition that has armed us mightily against other beasts, we turn upon ourselves. Visions of agony, of horrible prolonged suffering, unfold and proliferate behind the scripted scenes of our daily lives. For the sake of commerce, we dismiss them; yet at 4 a.m., exhausted but sleepless, we shiver while the devil scrapes his fiddle over us.

You have heard me tell the story of Sherlock Holmes (*Note: Eighteen weeks after this speech, authorities recovered a battered copy of* His Last Bow: Some Reminiscences of Sherlock Holmes *from the crime scene*), in which the detective performs an experiment. To discover how a murder was done, he seals himself at the crime scene, whereupon he and his assistant experience the sinister effects of a West African root extract called the devil's foot. When inhaled, the drug works by stimulating the brain centers that control the emotion of fear, thereby driving the victim mad with terror or frightening him to death. But while Watson hastens their escape from the chamber, we can never free ourselves from our own naturally occurring version of the devil's foot. Instead, we must live with our milder narcotic, moving through a reality inked and fused with shadows of horror. That we have devised strategies for enduring this is nature's way of seeing we prolong our stay on earth a while longer.

But I say it's madness, children, to continue in this manner. Madness to distract ourselves with ambition and fancy every day and take our dose of the devil's foot every night. What we do in these mountains is nothing more than the artist's countermeasure of sneaking up on this madness, this tragic state of affairs where we humans carry impure meals within ourselves, foul matter we cannot disgorge. For we too have the word "Meal" carved into our brows, someday to be sucked up by another sharer of life's burdens.

Every animal senses it will someday be nature's meal in one form or another, but we must wonder what it all means, and what may follow. It is into this pool of anxious speculation that we, you and I, wade with sympathy and compassion for all victims of creation. In our painted faces and tattered costumes we meet our panic, squeeze its shoulder and disarm it with a rueful smile.

So, who is mad? We who do this, or those who would change every disquieting thought or experience into a fantasy?

Some of you have queried why it is my friend (*Note: MC's top lieu-tenant, born Nicholas Drake Shirley, 1982*) and I have borrowed the names Cesare and Caligari. What does that cinematic duo have to do with the Tragedy House? You wonder if I am serious in showcasing my friend nightly in the large open cabinet beside me, keeping him heavily sedated and under hypnosis for the purpose of eliciting prophecies. Do I believe my companion's predictions? Or is this merely performance?

The answer is both. It is genuine but also theatrical, with a grand end in view. I have said as artists we approach our subject sneakily. Through kind words and gentle arts, we convince our man to put down his weapons and let the world go on without him. Our man is, of course, the cosmic panic that torments us. Of course, we cannot let him wander off over the horizon, but must accompany him on his journey. For we are joined to this man. To his loneliness. To his despair when he turns his thoughts toward the future and perceives a world without him, wondering what the shadows hold in store.

That is what draws me to prophecy; it is what makes me human. As it is with all men and women, my eyes are pinned to the curtain of death, my imagination spinning with pictures of what lies beyond it. You, too, children, if I haven't misjudged your shrewd caricatures upon the stage, hunger for a message of the future as you dance like flames around an open grave.

And so I command Cesare to open his eyes and peer into the future for us; hush, now, he speaks.

CESARE: Ye children of exile…

For nigh on six months we have dwelt on this mountain, transmuting our despair into bitter comedy. In fools' costume we have meditated on the step each must take after exhausting his clay in the repetitions of life. Gazing down into the valley (*Note: The nearest town is thirty miles north of the commune*), we see these repetitions mirrored in our counterparts, who move through a million poses, their progress an illusion of the longing that propels them. Estranged from the land, wretched mutants in the power they wield over it, they deceive themselves that their empires, their achievements, even their memories and desires, are as sword strokes cleaving through the fabric of blind forces.

It is thus, for self-deception is vital for survival. And we refrain from disillusioning them, knowing with what rancor we would be judged. Yet we withhold our own judgment, because we swing through the same repetitions, the same poses forced on us by terrestrial urgency. If only humanity had not been cursed to see through the marvel of animation to the empty gestures that organize its existence; then it could suffer its career as painlessly as a toymaker's experiment soon to be added to a heap of broken dolls.

Children of Caligari, we have promised you deliverance, and so you shall have it. This shelter finds us together for the last time. Salvation comes with a twist… a reversal of fortune conceived by your leader and me before we had ever guided you into these mountains and through the gates of the Tragedy House. But first you will know why we took the names Cesare and Caligari, and why we turned to an old German film for the following device.

One, it was right that your theatrical interests be embodied in a showman such as Caligari. Two, it was useful to imitate Caligari and offer Cesare as an instrument of prophecy. Three, it was advantageous to highlight the film's twist ending as a means of rejecting repression and also to prepare you through ritual predictions for what I am about to tell you… for we have reached the final act of the greatest performance we will ever give under these blind stars.

Brothers and sisters, at supper you were given tainted bread. The wafers you received contained a neurotoxin—our antidote to the devil's foot. It is through the powers of science that I predict you will all die within minutes, the result of your respiratory centers shutting down. My words will shortly have no meaning for you as you struggle—internally, for you may add paralysis to your ordeal—with the survival instincts that grip us to the end. You will die in the positions in which you took your seats, together with your leader and me, for recall we shared the same bread. Together we will be churned up and mashed into the bolus of pathos and despair that was once the Tragedy House, soon to be digested into the void.

Here, then, is your final prophecy: Behold Cesare, the Last Messiah. My voice issues the words of doom. They shall wrap thee like a shroud, weave like cloth over your millionth and last pose. May we cry for the kingdom of beasts and for our cousins in the valley, and smile as we trail like fading whispers into annihilation. For not only shall we be infertile, we shall lead our race's secret resistance to a world that offers us only poison and enslavement.

Now follow me into the darkness and the end of madness.

And may the universe forget us.

Amen.

CATCH YOU ON THE FLIP SIDE

I. Self

SOPHISTICATED SIPS E-ZINE

Full-bodied flash fiction for the online lit lover

Our electronic word java will stoke your cyber-soul. Grab a seat and let our signature blends transport you from your reading device to a psychic realm where a woman's laugh drives you insane and a bus ride takes you to the end of the night. We add flavor and finish to what T.S. Eliot called "the substratum of our being." And we will measure your life in coffee spoons.

Today's digital dose of belletristic brew:

SELF-PORTRAIT
By George Kuato

"God, look at that portrait," Lewis said.

"You talk as if it's horrid," Sylvia said.

"It's more than horrid. It's positively hideous. He's a swine in gentleman's clothes."

"Perhaps you're being harsh."

"Harsh? Humor me, Sylvia; try to see it through my eyes. Eyes...now that's where to start. How they glare at you, how they swipe at you like a scythe. Do you see it? The forehead taut, as if pricked with damnation; the horn of a beard, and the bushy brows that meet in the middle. That's damnation enough. And the bulbous nose that gives the face the shape of—why, you can almost hear him snorting, like an overgrown hog. Walk over this way; he's still staring at you. I think he would like to eat you."

"Stop it," Sylvia whispered, lowering her head.

"He must have been massive," Lewis pressed on, "so massive he stoops under his own weight. And wonderfully cunning in the effect he wished to produce. He had the picture hung at such a height over the landing so as to appear from below as though the master of the house himself, bandy-legged and huge in his black frock coat and top hat, were standing there measuring you with carnivorous lust.

"I have read of this man," he continued, slowing near the foot of the stairs, "a recluse who was disposed to treat his menials savagely in the fever-grip of drunkenness. I can imagine him, Sylvia (here—sit on this bench), hulking into classrooms at Edinburgh and thundering on the marvelous unbosomings of the corpse. He would terrify me and fascinate me all the same. I shouldn't think I could take my eyes off him."

"Oh, Lewis, can't we go back to the sitting room?"

"And listen to Polly's dreadful piano? Please, you're trying to observe with the same liberal consciousness that delights in your garden. Try to view the painting my way, like a cave dweller who perceives his own shadow in the gloom. For in my vision each shadow stands distinctly revealed, the shadow behind every shard of existence, preying on its own kind, mocking itself... But enough metaphysics. Back to the picture: Help me build it. Note the features, how they burn themselves on your mind's eye whether you regard the subject directly or not. They have a kind of sordid musical elegance about them which exhausts the limits of the grotesque. Our man is like a monstrous violin with a beard —no, no, that certainly won't do. He's like the shadow of a satyr in one of Baudelaire's brothels; no, wait a minute, rather like the creeping arm of the Marquis De Sade's nude, drooling ghost—"

"Lewis, please stop!"

He sighed, and sat on the bench beside her.

"You're only trying to provoke me," she said. "No man would allow himself to be depicted so."

"Ah, but I'm merely dispensing with the trivialities of, shall we say, surface delineation; speaking in truths of the heart."

"His heart? Is it so black, do you think?"

"I do think, Sylvia. Such a man has been stung by the viciousness of his peers. You can tell that—assuming the artist has been faithful—by the stamp of vengefulness on his brow. Left there in childhood, I would argue, for surely it would have taken him years to grow into those prominent features, which would have drawn accusations of wickedness in his youth. So that he would play the devil for survival's sake and find the role an unshakable one, even into adulthood."

"Then it's all a defense," she countered, "to close off an emptiness that might be filled by a loving woman."

He smiled, looking from her to the landing. "And that is why you captivate me, my dear: Those God-given lenses upon your face that allow you to spot a crack of light in even the darkest corners of the spirit. Yes, perhaps love might have worked on this man once."

"He doesn't seem so ugly now," she said.

There was silence a moment.

"But look," he broke out, turning to her, his eyes shining: "Beware, Sylvia, lest your scrupulous self-regard, your romantic invulnerability (which few, I dare say, have glimpsed beneath that haze of beneficence about you) should rouse that twisted creature on the landing, so that one day, one day he steps down from the portrait and with a noise like chunks of masonry hoisted with each step —*thump, thump, thump*—drooling like a fiendish monk—comes banging on your chamber door —"

She shrieked as his hand clamped on her arm.

"You're insufferable, Lewis," she said, rising.

"Am I? I was swept away by my conceit."

"I don't know why I play along with your games. They always end in some cruel joke."

With a barely audible huff she brushed her arm where he had touched her.

Then, with the hauteur of a dancer recovering from an inferior partner's stumble, she thrust out her elbow and waited; so remote and so beautiful, he thought, like a prisoner in a tower of gossamer and lace sculpted from ice.

He frowned, stroking his beard; then stood.

"Thanks to my 'scrupulous self-regard' as you call it," she said as they linked arms, "I asked Polly for a tour of the place before you came here. *And I know there is no portrait, but only a stained glass window on the landing.* A ballet of light and color so dazzling in her account of it that I ached to experience it as others do. Leave it to you, Lewis, to transform a celestial vision into something horrible for one who cannot see. Truths of the heart indeed."

And so saying she allowed the broad, bowed man to guide her down the hall.

II. Portrait

"It started off nicely," Brandon said. "But then it went on too long about how horrible the guy was. Overblown writing."

"Agreed," Keira said. "The writer could have trimmed some. But you've got to admit the twist ending was good."

"But was Lewis deliberately being cruel to Sylvia? Or just having a little fun to his way of thinking?" Vanessa scowled at her papers as she posed this to the Northwest Flash Fiction Freakazoids.

Consisting of nine aspiring writers at its peak, the group now stood at four. They met on campus as their schedules allowed to "dissect the use of brevity in the works of underpublished and emerging authors transmitting in all genres." Luke, the only published member, hated the smug, often over-long meetings. And yet he was the only Freakazoid who had attended every one.

Vanessa. His only motivation for enduring Brandon's discourses on Philip K. Dick. For making it to Medieval Literature every Tuesday and Thursday at eight in the morning. Half Irish, half Korean, she caught him off guard whenever she looked at him. Her curious brown eyes, so dark they seemed black, made him feel like a lumbering idiot, yet capable of change, as if he might emerge from his black-trench-coat-wearing, three-hundred-pound chrysalis to become someone semi-attractive, even desirable. Although he still wouldn't stand a chance with her.

Her romantic invulnerability.

"I think the story is deeper than it looks," he said. "It's all subtext, like Vanessa suggests."

"I'm not sure I'm suggesting that," Vanessa said.

Humor me, Vanessa; try to see it through my eyes.

"Yeah, Luke, clarify."

Luke turned to Keira across the table. But his attention burned around the dream girl at the edge of his vision, a tantalizing vagueness like a naked woman flitting through a moonlit forest.

He cleared his throat.

"What I mean is, the style reflects the man's extravagant way of speaking to conceal his self-hatred. It's no coincidence the story reads like *The Picture of Dorian Gray.*"

"I think you're mistaking the author's long-windedness for characterization," Brandon said.

And I think you should eat Philip K.'s dick, you swine in Mr. Rogers clothes.

But before Luke could voice this opinion more tactfully, his cell phone dinged.

"Get home if you're not already," read the incoming text message preview on his lock screen. Luke Sr., the deus ex machina of malcontent Freakazoids. "Well guys, it looks like I've been summoned."

"Laters," Brandon said.

"Peace," Keira said.

"Catch you on the flip side, Luke," Vanessa said, not looking up as she shuffled her papers.

"So much for George Kuato," Luke heard from Keira as he lingered a moment outside the classroom.

He stared at his size-13 combat boots as he rode the bus home.

So much for George Kuato was right. He shouldn't have submitted his story to the group under false pretenses. A literary vignette like "Self-Portrait"—despite its publication in an esteemed online litmag—was bound to leave the others cold. In Dewey Hall in Room 213 whenever the four could meet, depth took a back seat to plot twists and outrageous concepts. The girls thought he was hot shit ever since he took Advanced Fiction Writing. With Brandon leading the meetings, even Henry Miller would fall flat.

Another rub was the group's digital skimming habits. Vanessa was the only one besides Luke who read hard copy. And even she only vaguely sensed what "George Kuato" had accomplished. In under a thousand words, Luke's poetic double had used dialogue almost exclusively to depict a man's inner conflict and create irony and exaggeration so potent that it seemed as if the story was overwritten when really it illuminated the dark corners of Lewis's spirit.

Look into the dark corners of my spirit, Vanessa.

The retracting pneumatic bus doors sounded like a sigh.

Luke walked the five blocks from the bus stop to his house. The foyer still smelled of last night's ruined quiche, as well as the beef ravioli his dad had heated up after dumping Luke's experiment in the garbage. Luke Sr., the deus ex machina of Chef

Boyardee. He hurried up the stairs. His dad's work boots—size 13s, like his—weren't by the coat rack, which meant he still had a few minutes to surf porn.

Down in the living room, Paula stopped her daily torture marathon of "Ode to Joy" on the Steinway to catch her brother's tread on the landing. The stained-glass window there, with its yellows and blues and reds refracting midafternoon sunlight, so frightening after he watched *Suspiria* when he was ten, now only made him squint into its geometric conundrum impatiently. He locked himself in his room and plopped into his chair at his desktop computer.

His cell phone dinged. "Hitching a ride in five," read the incoming text message preview. The old man's daytime texts were as terse as his evening diatribes were expansive. Another ding. "Make dinner. No vegetarian."

Luke silenced his cell phone. Time to pull up his online obsession—Lillian Chong.

She was Vanessa's dead ringer on SploogeTube, only border-line anorexic. His favorite video of her was a POV, a dude with Lou Ferrigno forearms giving her a cream pie. The HD stream made it easy for him to fall into the illusion of banging Lillian Chong missionary style. Whenever Luke masturbated to the video, fighting for leverage against his big thighs and belly—like giving a polar bear a reach-around—the porn star would morph in his mind's eye. She would become Vanessa, legs spread wide, nipples needle-stiff, totally going Freakazoid under his vicarious Incredible Hulk thrusts.

"Oh God, Vanessa," Luke would rasp in hoarse delight, as "Ode to Joy" screeched through the floor like a tone-deaf cheer and sperm shot past the Angel Soft toilet tissue he pressed to his dick to slick a crevice (once even the Apple logo on his monitor) in his keyboard.

And that is why you captivate me, my dear.

While he accessed the website, he imagined a text from her.

"I knew it was your story," punctuated with a winking eye and stuck-out tongue emoji. "Only you would write such a deep, sexy piece and then credit it with an Arnold Schwarzenegger movie reference. Ha ha, Kuato. I love-love-LOVE *Total Recall*. But I love you even more, Luke, I wish you were here with me. I want you deep inside me."

The POV video took time loading. Dimly visible, Luke's reflection stared back at him from the black monitor.

I'm starting to look like Dad, he thought. Someday I'll look just like him.

His monobrow furrowed.

Vanessa—is this what you see when you look at me?

Could you spot a crack of light in the dark corners of my spirit?

Catch you on the flip side, Luke.

The repulsive face faded as the video finally began playing. But an impressionistic ghost remained, arrested behind Lillian Chong's rolling eyes and protruding ribs. Luke grabbed his sperm wipe and brutalized his cock. Yes, you will, Vanessa, he thought, as his sylvan goddess emerged from her Lillian Chong chrysalis in the zone of illusion between the flat screen in front of him and his synapses.

You'll catch me on the flip side, Vanessa.

When I step down from the portrait and come banging on your chamber door.

O MOTHER GODDESS, WHERE ART THOU?

God, it's dark in here. Where am I? It seems to me I've wandered into some strange places.

I don't remember. No, I do remember something. I was stroking keys at a computer… a daily habit. Sometimes it resulted in a check that came to my door. The earnings were primarily spent at a bar called The Heavenly Hole.

But maybe I'm wrong. Maybe I've never been to a place called The Heavenly Hole. Maybe I heard that name from somewhere else. All I clearly remember is I was typing. Words accumulated on my computer screen, something in the nature of a fantasy. The subject turned to an establishment called The Angels Club.

Further key strokes revealed advertisements in a blacked-out window:

ADVENTURES OF THE WEIRD
HOUSE OF NIGHT AND MYSTERY
A LOVER'S APOCALYPSE
JOURNEY TO THE END OF IMAGINATION
REALLY, REALLY, REALLY, REALLY NAKED GIRLS!

One passerby, well on in years, steps into this emporium of delights. Roused from daydream or worry or nothing at all, he finds himself inside a cold, low-ceilinged lobby. His body feels like a dingy old coat, the sum of his faded summers and sour winters of remembering, which circumstance has placed before a topless woman coming toward him. He didn't see her emerge from anywhere, nor can he recall having ever gazed upon such luscious fruit.

He actually thinks: Luscious fruit.

You're handsome, she says. *I could eat you up*.

Oh, but this is degrading into pretense. I may as well out myself rather than keep posing as someone else... some other needy grandpa hoping to unzip for a lady not interested in urine samples.

I'm gaping at this woman as if I'm having a stroke. She looks like the earth's core dreamed her into being. Like the priestess of some lost tribe in an erotic Tarzan novel. An interesting comparison, seeing how I've never read a Tarzan novel. She takes my hand and kisses it. The hand that applies hemorrhoid cream to my anus. That waters the thirsty angels at The Heavenly Hole. Speaking of which—but she lowers my proctologically diligent, Mastercard-ready hand, watering postponed.

The priestess motions me into a hallway past a rice paper wall. Her wake breathes rose and musk. The corridor runs straight for some two hundred yards with doors on both sides. An electric pink radiance fills it like mist, or a hologram of mist, giving off no cold or moisture.

Finally she stops at a door. Black with symbols chalked in the same lurid pink, interlocking circles and triangles.

She says, with phone-sex breathiness, *We are not a normal massage parlor.*

I don't admit this, but I think: Whatever, I've wandered into strange places before. Once I found myself on a neighbor's jungle gym at two in the morning in a downpour. What happens when your brain cells settle in one for long drunk at the Alzheimer's Lodge.

I push the door open. Halfway in it sticks on the plush carpet. The smells of lotion and sweat create a dismal impression of normal. The kind of normal I miss… not then, in the Angels Club—but here, in this abyss, or wherever I am now, cut off from reference points. A cobweb on a radiator, any humdrum detail to demystify the purgatory that has been holding me for who knows how long.

It's even taken my name from me. Call me XXXX on the tip of my tongue.

I'm in a vestibule. That's the association that arises. The word predicates a position preliminary to something holy. I've done something wrong. This absolute darkness presses on me like guilt. It has the finality of judgment, of grace beyond knowing.

I'm sitting in a black vestibule. I say sitting, but I have no bones. No connective tissues, no nerves, no blood, no breath. I don't feel my legs, my groin, there was always such tension down there. I don't feel my neck or eyeballs. I feel oddly naked not blinking or wanting to pee. Something, my name included, is being hidden from me. My gutless gut tells me this place is a Band-aid on a wound I shouldn't see.

Still, I want to see. I can ask this vestibule—this cage for all practical reasons—questions. How can I ask questions and not feel my pubic bone? Give me tangibles…

The Angels Club room had bare white walls. Dirty blinds, a ficus plant near one corner. I stood in the middle of the room with my pants down. My priestess was really, really, really, really naked now and cruel as a medieval torturer. She would suck me off to the edge, then release me, achingly stiff, and study me with a tight smile. When she focused on my glans, her eyes crossed slightly.

The imperfection excited me. So did her hands. She would have had to be six feet tall to match their size. Yet they were beautiful, only my mother's hands approached such elegance. Only in this bodiless state would I think of my mother in the context of a blow job. The cold, that's why I made the connection. The priestess's hands were icy as though she'd been stocking a milk cooler. Like my mother's hands when I went to her viewing.

I couldn't resist—when no one was looking I lifted the top one resting on her lower abdomen. It had the heavy, yielding character of refrigerated fascia and bone.

Talk about a conversation stopper. The boundaries had really shifted between us, hadn't they? A childish thought... it has the virtue of being heartfelt.

There I was. Standing over my mother in a new button-up shirt, this woman who had wiped my ass and who now gave me nothing more than a sneer from the velvet-flooded silver barge she'd picked for a casket. That's as good as it gets sometimes. Death begets bromides. The total surrender of her stone hand in mine restored me, though.

I draped the hand over its partner. Having sampled the goods so to speak, I now saw my mother's hands as impersonal objects. The crescent moons at the nail bases, the wrinkling around the knuckles. The slight cupping gesture in pronation. Those are the hands of Bergman, I thought. The artist. He told such moving stories through his hand drawings. Hands in affection, hands in violence, hands isolated, joined, searching... Shouldn't have told Bergman.

"Old pervert," he said when I confided in him, no, that's not what he said. We were in someone's living room.

People stood around drinking beer. The smell of beef stew wafted in from the kitchen. Somehow I went from telling Bergman about a story I was working on to my mother's viewing. How I had looked at her and thought, "Jackson Bergman would draw her hands." The artist grimaced like I'd shown him a turd. "No," he said. He sat in a wooden chair against the wall. He looked paler than I'd ever seen him. He squeezed his knees and walked off.

Perhaps I shouldn't have steered the conversation like that. Not everyone wants you to make a confession. Even if you don't mean to, you encroach on their boundaries. Their natural response is to retreat to a familiar thought pattern. In my case, Bergman retreated from the room.

But isn't that why I'm in this nothingness? To confess? To remember what I need to confess? Why all the fuss about my mother's hands? The last question prompts a foreign thought as if my cage has decided to speak to me. Knowledge flows into my brain, the shadowy remnant aboard this Cartesian express to nowhere, *I-Think-Therefore-I-Amtrak*.

The woman in the casket was not my mother.

That woman was at least seventy, younger than me. I don't recall who she was or why I was at her viewing or why I touched the hand of someone else's deceased mother. And how do I know Jackson Bergman? I'm not a writer and I don't know any artists. I was a landscaper for more years than Bergman has been alive. My cage-granted wisdom tells me Bergman is not quite forty. I can only conclude these are not my memories. They belong to a Bergman acquaintance, someone his own age.

"Look at that old pervert."

Yes, that's me—old pervert.

I'm at least eighty. No wonder I like the priestess's crossed eyes, the imperfection connects us. That and her big, foxy hands, cold as death. Her right hand tugged at my erection, alternated with flicks of her tongue which was yellowish and waxy. No—that was the Italian whore's tongue. The whore I saw more than once in my Army days. She had the crossed eyes and elegant hands.

The Italian whore gave expert head. Her breath was bad, that was the problem. Like rancid cooking. The priestess was not the Italian whore. My bones did not ache when I was young. I came twice in a row with the Italian whore. A neat way to spend your R & R. But the other woman, the priestess, she would take me to the edge and tension would shoot from the base of my pelvis to the top of my head like I was performing a strict sit-up. My old knees ached, they weren't used to the weight of my trunk bearing straight down on my thighs. My toes digging into the orthotic in-soles of my loafers.

The woman in the casket looked like an older version of the Italian whore.

I'm no longer sure who any of these women are anymore. I miss the chronic ache in my pelvis, the strain on my lumbar region, the affirmations of who I was. A landscaper.

I'd planted bulbs for a friend, a journalist, who took me for a beer later. At a place called The Heavenly Hole. It might not have been called The Heavenly Hole, but that's how I see the electric pink neon sign, minus the last two letters which had burned out: THE HEAVENLY HO. Two-dollar specials on oyster shooters. Inside, bass notes shook the walls, rude elbows, beer breath. We sat at a stage where a woman with slightly crossed eyes and dark hair slid down a pole in a floating ballerina pose. Then she went to the stage front and propped her seven-inch heel on my shoulder. My smiling muscles cramped around my gums.

"Look at that old pervert," someone said, two seats down.

The young man grinned in the stage mirror, his eyes like someone photographed in mid-blink, his hair in a pompadour with the sides shaved into lines. The stripper bent toward my friend on my other side. No, he wasn't my friend, I didn't know him. I'd thought, earlier that day, about Jackson Bergman and how we'd had lunch at a strip club the last time I saw him. He told me he planned to climb a water tower that evening to capture the view for a book he was illustrating. His obituary said he died of "injuries suffered in a fall." After I'd planted the bulbs, I thought, "I should go to a strip club and have a drink in honor of Jackson Bergman." Now this prick with a scurvy haircut doing what I'm doing, admiring a naked woman and calling me a pervert. Presumably because I'm not young.

Well, I'm not. I have conflicting memories. Too many years of fantasy and reality and dream and memory have gotten all tangled up. I can't compute them anymore.

But a blow job… that computes.

My priestess, infernal head-giver, takes me to the edge again and I feel either a fart or a faint, maybe both, coming on. Then for the fourth or fifth time, she stops.

Wouldn't it be nice to let go, she says. The woman is crueler than April. Of course, I say, if you would let me, you bitch. All but the bitch part. We both laugh. My smiling muscles are getting extra work today. Then I remember I don't like how I look when I smile.

I don't like my face. It shouldn't be seen smiling. It has sunken eyes and thin lips and something flinching about it. No woman should see a visage like that scrunching toward orgasm. It's as ugly as this room with dirty blinds. As ugly as the Italian whore's breath. Recalling this, my opinion of my face, prompts another message from the cage. Its language is concrete, like a parable or nightmare. It has no need for transitions, perhaps because it's all transition. And the end point.

I am transported to a narrow, windowless room. The walls and floor are cedar. Coats and backpacks line both sides. The bench beneath me is too deep to rest my back against the rear wall. Silence. Despite its trappings, this place has an underlying austerity, the hint of a vast, indefinite withholding. Hence the feeling of more than five paces separating me from the barrel of rubber balls by the door.

This will be another lunch hour without dodgeball, I think.

I've done something wrong.

I am waiting to be released. Wouldn't it be nice to let go? Of course, if you would let me... but first I have to find out what I've done. The door opens. Miss Stinkface walks in. She is why I am in this room full of coats and backpacks and rubber balls. She is the one who keeps me here during the lunch hour. Miss Stinkface has black, feathered hair. She is pretty. Even when she nails me with a hard look and her eyes cross slightly. She stands over me wearing a long-sleeved silver blouse, a shell necklace of some unearthly green, and white polyester bell bottoms. Her perfume smells of rose and musk. She has long, precise fingers... fingers Jackson Bergman would draw.

Right now she's pointing at my face and grimacing. Her breath smells like rancid cooking. I avert my eyes to the crucifix above the door.

This cloakroom is preliminary to something holy. No it's not, it's preliminary to recess. I am waiting to be released. "You are not the center of attention," Miss Stinkface says. Not for the first time. Her real name won't come to me, but I know she dislikes my enthusiasm in class, my free spirit, I think she's called it. It encroaches on her space. Or maybe it's my face she objects to. Whatever the case, she responds by handing out anti-bromides.

She says, at this moment, shaking her finger at me, "The world is not all about you." I don't remember what I've done this time.

No, I do. I raised my hand to answer a question. When she didn't call on me I let it fall to my desk too quickly, a mischievous complaint made with wood and bone. "Look at me," Miss Stink-face says, snapping my attention from the crucifix, "you are not the center of attention, Tobin Malone." So many n's in that sentence, like a succession of doors banging shut.

She's right, I'm not the center of attention. I'm one of thirteen students in the second grade at Our Lady of Devotion. Yet she has singled me out. She pays a great deal of attention to my being unworthy of attention. And the contradiction, this stupid conflicting message, has dominated my attention ever since. For example, my facial inferiority complex. But who is this Miss Stinkface anyway? Who is this unruly student, Tobin Malone? I haven't been a boy since Franklin Roosevelt was in office.

Wouldn't it be nice to let go?

Yes, I say. Yes. Then I can shed the fantasies and realities and dreams and memories of too many years of computing and be reborn into Tobin Malone.

Malone would be half my age. Apparently he writes fiction, probably bad fiction. Pulp stuff. His most traumatic memory is being scolded by his second-grade teacher in the cloakroom. That and moving the hand of his dead mother. The cage assures me the woman in the casket was his mother. With a twist: Rejection came first. Doesn't it always? Bromides. Malone was given up at birth. There was a woman before the woman in the casket. He never felt this first woman's hands, they never touched him. He was delivered and promptly removed.

Malone remembers now. The delivery room, the cloakroom,

the viewing room, all places that say, "You are not the center of attention." As he remembers I forget, who I am and why I came to this room with the dirty blinds.

My memory is deteriorating. Whatever, I've wandered into strange places before.

Strange and tormenting.

Wouldn't it be wonderful, she says, my priestess, *to be free and to remember and know nothing?* I am so close to coming now I would agree to anything. *To live in an eternal feeling of reaching toward something? Not waiting, but reaching?* Yes, yes, YES, I nod. I've just choked off the first spurts of orgasm. I wonder if this is what Jackson Bergman felt like the moment he lost his footing on the water tower.

She shines her eyes at me as if eager to watch me grow wings and take flight.

Then let's finish this, she says.

My pelvic muscles dance like Wile E. Coyote at the apex of a long drop. When I get close again, she stops.

Goddamn bitch, I say. All but the bitch part.

I have to stoop down to hear what she says next. The boundaries have really shifted between us, haven't they? A childish thought, it has the virtue of being heartfelt. Oh, my priestess is cruel — and full of advice.

Keep your eyes on the ficus plant, she says. *You'll see it's not a plant, but something else. The interdimensional gateway to the Aeon of Daphnos, the mother goddess. Marshall all your intention toward it.*

I'm marshalling intention all right, at least five milliliters' worth. It's going to tarnish my priestess's lustrous black hair if she doesn't stop talking. She's telling me about the moment of sexual release which not even she can stem at this point.

When you release your seed, she says, *your terrestrial nature will cease. Your astral body will pass into the Forever Corridor. This will deliver you to the Aeon of Daphnos. Once you cross over, you will become part of her. But be careful. The Evil One, haunter of the corridor, who calls himself Sardonikei, will try to trap you. He will use the language of the ego to make you his prisoner. You must have no words, do you hear me,*

NO WORDS in your astral consciousness once you are inside the corridor. The corridor itself is the Word and will permit of no others.

Or what would happen, I want to ask, if I could squeeze sounds from my throat. But the urge to squeeze is all down below.

This is it, I feel it. My priestess is done tormenting me. I fix my eyes on the ficus plant as she asked. Forever is only five paces away. Now that I know this, the illusion dissolves. Where a ficus plant had been stands a column made of hands, beautiful, precise hands such as Jackson Bergman would draw.

Hands reaching out like thirsty angels—my predecessors, wretched men like me.

I will join them.

Only, don't think. There must be no words when I leave my physical form. Or what? I can't help it, all those n's echo in my mind as I prepare to leave the creaky suspension system I called my body. Confession. Attention. Rejection. Jackson. Bergman. TOBIN MALONE flashes in my mind's eye and I wonder how he's doing. He is remembering and I am disintegrating, he is my rebirth he is not the center of attention and yet he is my attention and I am *"No words,"* the priestess says. Ribbons of semen paste her hair as my astral being enters the Forever Corridor.

I am flying through darkness. The whip-fire sensations of my last orgasm, the climax of climaxes, disperse in the Grand Unifying Theory of Tobin Malone. Behind the immensity of that idea sounds the imbecilic snort-laugh of what can only be Sardonikei, the Evil One.

I've been metaphysically punked. My astral stomach drops. I'm falling from a water tower at the summit of the universe. My wings have failed me at an altitude close to heaven and there is no earth to stop me, only a hole forgotten by forever, the trap the priestess had warned me about. The last proprioceptive ghost of my disembodied senses is extinguished by the slamming of an unseen door.

TOBIN MALONE,

he is not here, there is no one in here,
only me. In this black vestibule, this cloakroom cage
of pure thought with nothing to do but pay
attention to itself. I can't escape, I can do
nothing but wait. Whatever, I've
wandered into strange places
before... but where am I?
It seems to me I've

...

HOOD SIGIL

A tribute to the signs in my neighborhood

I'm thankful for everyone
love everyone
God is most glorified in us
when we are most satisfied
in Him

STOP

we will be closed March 31
(Easter)
Jesus is nowhere
harden the fuck up

drive like your kids live here
end the monster houses
no more condos
God is most glorified in us
when we are most satisfied in

Tito's Handmade Vodka

end the
no more
like your kids
monster God
drive condos

love is most glorified when we
harden the fuck up

Tito's Jesus
Easter monster
fuck your kids
fuck your condos
fuck up thankful
fuck Him
fuck everyone
live in vodka

closed
like love

STOP

drive

be glorified
be handmade
be thankful
be like your kids
be nowhere
be satisfied

drive

THE RAEKWONOMICON

Every hero's tale deserves a prologue.
— The Raekwonomicon

He comes from the League of SorceRZAs in the 36th dimension. The sorceRZAs are masters of mystical chessboxing. They fight The Hidden — the things under reality's stairs created by the Shadow Mastaz, the Shaolin's most powerful magicians.

War is the equalizer, the Dao of the Wu-niverse.

Today's battlefield is Earth. The sorceRZA makes the drop like an occult paratrooper. He starts as vapor, then grows flesh when he touches down. His mission is to track Shaolin movement in The Crawl, an urban hell where the dead lie unburied and the living skulk in the ruins of corrupt politics and economic stagnation. The Crawl is essentially an above-ground cemetery with accommodations for criminals, lunatics and fugitives.

His last defense is his "double," a self-replicating unit on the astral plane that individuates through metabolic growth if needed.

In a few hours, it will be needed.

Things are about to get messy for Ol' Dirty Wan.

A sorceRZA sees the enemy within.
— The Raekwonomicon

In true form, the sorceRZA out-danced opponents like a 36th-dimension Ali. But in the mundane ring he had two left feet, his human orb's limbic system slow to process the uncanny.

So though his meta-gut screamed *Danger, Will Robinson*, he gawked at the kid whose moans had drawn him from shelter after dusk. The gangly teenager was scrambling up a telephone pole with ninja speed. Six feet up, Ninja Boy froze, monkey-hugging the moonlit pole.

Something moved under his grass-stained Carmelo Anthony jersey. Ol' Dirty Wan's instincts prayed a desperate *I'm Audi*, but his orb stayed frozen.

The A and Y of the jersey bulged out like vanilla popsicles. Under the popsicles an *Alien*-burst ruptured through his back in a V formation of long, chitinous stalks that ended in disco ball-sized globes. The kid looked like a junkie mutant cherub wrapped around the telephone pole, one wing high above Ol' Dirty Wan's face.

In human form Ol' Dirty Wan called himself Chuck Morgan.

Morgan's heart skipped a beat when the globes burped ash.

They snowed down on him, and he saw they were more like tiny white petals. Finally Ol' Dirty Wan found the right neuron circuit and sent Morgan back into the building he had come from. He closed his eyes and meditated on his third eye. From his internal viewing room — which resembled a parlor with a mantel bearing his aura shield — he examined his circulatory system and found an unwanted guest.

He went to the shield and drew a cloaking sigil to deflect Shaolin mind readers.

Then he mentally hailed the intruder.

Stronger than the fist is the power to conversate.
— The Raekwonomicon

I see you. Explain yourself.

EAT A DICK.

You have something to do with the boy on the telephone pole?

EEYUUHHHHUHHHUHHHUHHH

Cooperate or I'll raise my healing vibration.

HA, THAT STUFF'S FOR SUCKERS.

Not so.

OWWWW!!! OKAY, RESPECT FOR THE REIKI FINGAZ. WHAT YOU WANT?

What are you?

I'M A PARASITICAL FUNGUS. I PRODUCE A SPORE THAT MANIPULATES THE HUMAN BRAIN. WHEN PEOPLE INGEST ME THEY TURN INTO ZOMBIE SLAVES AND SPREAD ME AROUND LIKE NOROVIRUS. I'M LIKE JANET JACKSON, MAKIN' MY OWN ZOMBIE RHYTHM NATION.

Why?

SAME REASON FUNGI LIKE ME PREY ON ANT COLONIES HERE ON EARTH. IT'S THE DAO. CH-CHICK-POW!

Who's behind this?

NAH, I AIN'T GOIN' THERE...

Who?

OWWWWWW!!! ENOUGH WITH THE WOO WOO SQUEEZE! YOUR BROTHER, AIIGHT? MYND RECKA.

You speak the truth. You may go.

OH THANK YOU BOSS, THANK YOU. I'M A DEPART NOW. BUT YOU AND ME, WE AIN'T DONE. IN 24 HOURS I'M BRINGIN' SOME HARD, PIPE HITTIN', BRAIN CELL EATIN' NIGGAS. THE DEATH DREAM ANGEL IS GETTING MEDIEVAL ON YOUR —

Ol' Dirty Wan closed his mental viewing room, preserving the sigil on his aura shield.

He looked down at the junkie mutant cherub clenched around the telephone pole beneath the second-story window.

The road to salvation is fraught with illusion.
— The Raekwonomicon

Ol' Dirty Wan walked into the brownfield on The Crawl's south side. The Stink was three miles of mothballed contamination that used to give wayfarers tumors. The barren landscape reflected his thoughts. He saw only one way to avoid becoming the Death Dream Angel's zombie slave — place his orb in permanent quarantine.

He looked around at the other unwitting victims streaming from The Crawl. The Death Dream Angel was directing them to the surrounding communities. Nothing, not even bodily destruction, could prevent their transformation into biological weapons. His brother, Mynd Recka, was the Shaolin's top pestilence maker. He created infectious diseases and plagues like the military built Humvees.

"You've got a sickness, man," his brother told him in the Battle of Liquid Swords on Neptune. "You're like that hippie sorceRZA from Nazareth — hurting yourself for suckers, bleeding for the sake of bleeding."

If bleeding maintained the cosmic balance, Ol' Dirty Wan would bleed till the end of time.

The time for his orb would come much sooner, though. By sunrise Morgan would resemble Ninja Boy. Already he had a cough, like his fellow travelers, which The Stink, long considered safe for passage, could not account for. He had visions, too, photographically distinct impressions of Vanessa crawling toward him. His old girlfriend was nude and filthy, with dead leaves in her hair. Each time she collapsed on the prickly grass before she could reach him. Chitinous stalks burst from her spine.

She looked like an angel who had jumped off her cloud because her wings were useless and revolting. This was Mynd Recka's modus operandi, a looped waking nightmare meant to shake him through his mind's eye.

"Man, you look like you've seen a ghost."

Zombie Vanessa vanished. In her place stood a ruddy,

balding man with a dirty bandage around his left thumb. Craggy muscles glistened with sweat under his overalls. "We all have, right? Come on, I know where we can catch a ride. I'll drop you anywhere's south of here."

Ol' Dirty Wan pitied the doomed man, who had a gap in his front teeth.

"That would be great. I'm in a bit of a hurry, actually."

Our ultimate goal is disarmament.
— The Raekwonomicon

Not all the wanderers were infected. "Mac" turned out to be a parasite himself, a sexual vampire. Together with two men lying in wait he attacked Ol' Dirty Wan outside an abandoned factory. The sorceRZA took down the gang-rapists with Tiger Style kung fu.

He should have run a mind scan on Mac first, but Vanessa's phantasm had rattled him. He told himself to stay focused while he drove his psychokinetically hotwired pickup truck out of The Stink. Outside Tical, the nearest town, he ran out of gas. Walking into town, he sent out psychical feelers.

"That's how you locate the enemy," his brother told him before the Schism. "A warrior stays focused by transferring mental anguish to his double. This causes a cosmic energy shift — a kind of heat signature. You project personally disturbing imagery to the suspected area and read for fluctuations."

Ol' Dirty Wan let the trauma of "seeing" a crawling-dead Vanessa dissolve in his orb. He had taught himself to absorb emotions organically, knowing his brother's tactics.

His own psychical feelers operated in reverse. He showed Tical's residents a world without The Crawl and men like Mac. Where food abounded and citizens greeted each other on the street. Feasts ran for days, wine flowed, stories were told and the sun rose and set in smog-free plumage. His images worked beneath conscious perception, to avoid valuations that might dim the collective energy he wanted to use.

Associations outside his control faded in. People smiling,

animals playing… loving memories of the departed. The towns-people's unconscious affection emitted a golden light which Ol' Dirty Wan drew into a telepathic sigil upon a B-17 bomber plane mounted on blocks in the town square. The de-weaponized memorial fit his intention behind the sigil.

"Help me find a gravedigger."

Cash rules everything around me. This is true in all universes.
— The Raekwonomicon

The midday sun blazed down on Tical. Odors of struggle choked the hot streets like the stink of emotional compost bins.

Ol' Dirty Wan's psychical feelers had nourished the towns-people's energy bodies. But the physical ones still sagged under their burdens. His best option was a big kid with meth sores outside a convenience store. He took one glance back at the bomber spreading its dead wings over the cityscape. Then he walked toward the tweaker.

Before he could speak, the ground shook.

BOOOOOMMM. BOOOOOMMM. Like ghost pilots attacking Tical with its landmark. Ol' Dirty Wan turned the corner toward the source. Down the street, inside a garage, a man lifted a barbell from the floor and returned it. The crash rocked the block. He turned away and clasped his hands behind his shaved head. Tattooed across his broad brown back was the word SARDONICAZ.

Ol' Dirty Wan scanned the man's mind. He saw acute aware-ness of death and empathy for the sick. And books. The covers were cartoon drawings. They showed headless corpses, men in pig masks and beasts with *Brobdingnagian* erections. Under the titles was the word in his tattoo.

A writer, he thought. Imaginative.

Morbidly inclined.

Able-bodied.

Play it smart.

"Mr. Sardonicaz?"

"Ha, no. Name's Curtis. How can I help?"

Curtis's smile was an eggshell over his aggression toward the tall, shabbily dressed stranger in his driveway. Speaking softly, Ol' Dirty Wan presented himself as eccentric millionaire, Chuck Morgan.

"I'm the founder of Ol' Dirty Fitness. You've heard of it? No? Well, anyway, I have a proposition."

Seated on a bench in Curtis's sweltering garage, he made it.

"Just so I understand," Curtis said. "You want me to bury you in a coffin in The Stink?"

"Nine feet deep," Chuck Morgan said.

"Then leave you?"

"Like I said, I'm an escape artist. It's part of my workout."

"You've got a coffin?"

"Your town must have a mortuary."

"What about transport?"

"A pickup truck. It needs gas, though."

"Don't take this the wrong way, Mr. Morgan, but I have a hard time believing you're a millionaire fitness guru."

Chuck Morgan grabbed the barbell and pulled it to standing. Then he set it down and handed Curtis several C-notes from his jeans pocket.

"You didn't just do that. Lift six-hundred pounds one-handed."

"And I didn't just give you enough C.R.E.A.M. to buy yourself a mode of transport."

"My niece needs it more. She's going through chemo and my loser-ass brother won't help with medical costs. Fine, you've got a gravedigger." Curtis extended his hand. "Funny. I write books under a pen name. Sardonicaz, like my tattoo says. It's inspired by a fictional character who goes insane after he digs up his father's corpse."

Meditation exists to help Ol' Dirty (M.E.T.H.O.D.).
— *The Raekwonomicon*

Chuck Morgan waited in the driveway while Curtis biked to the highway with a gas can. Curtis returned with the pickup and stowed the bike in the garage. They bought a casket at the town mortuary. Morgan paid extra to avoid inquiries.

The bribe, like Curtis's C-notes, was an illusion. But so was all money. C.R.E.A.M. existed because people agreed to believe in it. Ol' Dirty Wan was protecting them from an apocalyptic infection by manipulating the fantasy. That was how he rationalized deceiving men like Curtis. If he came out of this, he would tell Curtis his powers, which reached even into cyberspace. Curtis would be devastated, but he would know the truth. His paranoid energy would reflect reality rather than the conundrum of a stranger who frightened him.

Morgan bought supplies at a hardware store. Then they drove into The Stink.

They parked near the abandoned factory. Mac and his accomplices were gone. Curtis sat on the tailgate and chomped on a sub.

"I'm gonna lay this on the table and then shut up," he said. "First, my dream: You're the real deal. I couldn't find anything about you on the Internet, but that doesn't mean you aren't about to do something amazing. A strongman escape artist built like Jimmie Walker? Man, you should have a reality show.

"Second, my nightmare: This is your elaborate way of rolling up on me and you've read too much Edgar Allan Poe."

"If it makes you feel better," Chuck said, "meet me at the bomber at dawn. I'll tell you how I did it."

He'd meant to arrange the meeting with sigil magic, but Curtis's nerves were on edge.

While Curtis toiled with pick and shovel, Ol' Dirty Wan meditated. He returned to his third eye's viewing room. Next to the cloaking sigil on his aura shield he drew a cutting sigil to break his brother's connection with the fungus. He couldn't afford to let the two link since the Death Dream Angel had reached his brain.

When he woke from his trance, the sun had dipped behind the wall surrounding the new industrial complex to the west. A lone guard tower stood against the Martian-red sky. War was in the air. It called to Ol' Dirty Wan through the smog, The

Stink's rotten-egg stench, the steel-meets-dirt noise of Curtis's labors.

Could he avoid a mystical showdown with Mynd Recka?

His brother's psychical feelers took on the quality of a Japanese horror movie. Several times Vanessa's undead ringer climbed from the deepening grave and crawled toward him. In sunset's Grand Guignol hues, she perished in muted agony. Fungus wings *Alien*-burst from her back and rained spores upon the poisoned earth.

When Curtis had dug the hole to nine feet, Ol' Dirty Wan threw a rope down. He looked into the pit and wondered if he had the strength to transcend what it symbolized. Mynd Recka's Vanessa loop had exhausted him, and his orb's immune system had started a fever to fight infection. His powers were low. Still, he managed to move the rope psychokinetically while pretending to pull on it. Curtis climbed from the hole. His expression turned from admiration to dismay.

"The Stink doesn't seem good for you," he said.

Morgan started to reassure him, then burst out coughing.

They dropped the casket into the hole by moonlight. Morgan climbed down the rope, lifted the lid and stood inside. He stripped off his clothes, except for his briefs, and tossed them up to Curtis who laid them nearby.

"They get in the way," he said.

"You sure you want to go through with this?"

"I'm sure. But first tell me this: Who is Jimmie Walker?"

Sometimes one must bring the ruckus.
— The Raekwonomicon

Spiritually as well as physically, Ol' Dirty Wan was tired. His eons-long life had been spent battling the Shaolin. The darkness and sound of dirt hitting the casket soothed him. He wondered how it would feel to be eternally at peace, free from emotions he refused to shift onto his double or convert to martial energy like his brother.

But practice taught him to shut down his inner martyr. The

willingness to self-sacrifice that in its positive manifestation drove him to do the League's dirty work. Hence the name — Ol' Dirty Wan, who chased The Hidden through the slaughter-houses and sewers of reality to maintain the cosmic balance. He volunteered for the League's grimiest missions, often lethal ones for his orbs.

Despite his meta-level control, his body panicked. He calmed it with deep breaths and focused on his brow chakra. He called on light from Bobby Digital, his favorite star, to beam into an opening in the crown of his head. Then he created grounding cords, intangible energy tubes running from the base of his spine and major organs into the earth. Heaven and earth qi would stabilize him while the orb bore the physical brunt of mystical pugilism.

He opened his internal viewing room. The sigils on his aura shield were gone. In the back of the room was a door. It did not belong here. He turned the knob. He entered an apartment, his old place with Vanessa. Her books were stacked neatly on the nightstand and her clothes littered the floor. Frankincense burned on the dresser. On their wall bed a beefy blonde man was sodomizing her so hard the hinges rattled. He had paintball-red eyes and gold teeth.

"What up, bitch." The voice was the Death Dream Angel's.

He jerked Vanessa's head back. Her mascara ran from crying. She broke free and jumped out the window. Screams rang out four stories below.

Ol' Dirty Wan pointed at the grinning rapist. "You're not even a ghost."

The scene vanished in black smoke.

White light flickered. Now he was strapped to a chair in a room with stainless steel walls. A soiled mattress lay by the door. The overhead bulb faltered. By its weak light he read the upside-down words on the straitjacket binding him under his restraints: PROPERTY OF THE SHADOW MASTAZ. The door opened, and Vanessa crawled onto the mattress, nude and covered in semen. Her face was a sleepwalker's. The Death Dream Angel strode in after her, his limp penis dangling between his knees. Then Ol' Dirty Wan's near-spitting image entered, wearing a black trench coat.

"Nice cloaking job," Mynd Recka said. "It took me three counter-sigils to find you."

His partner threw up the Shaolin's S sign. "Told you I'd be back, dawg. I work faster when you irritate me."

Faintly, like distant thunder, Ol' Dirty Wan felt the vibrations of earth piling on his casket.

He said, "Let's do this."

Mynd Recka shed the trench coat. His prick stiffened to elephantine dimensions. "I've developed a new technique," he said.

"The Vlad Style." The Death Dream Angel stroked himself.

The pair resembled the monsters in Curtis's books.

Mynd Recka moved sullenly to the mattress. He was conserving energy. He had made a bold move preempting their mystical chessboxing ring. Ol' Dirty Wan recalled the Battle of the Cuban Linx Moon where his brother had exhausted all his power on illusions. His ego always betrayed him, like the heat signatures he studied. Still, he had turned Vanessa's memory into a potent thoughtform.

The Death Dream Angel launched into villain-monologue.

"So here we are in the Mystical Matrix. Only this artificial reality is twice as strong with my bacterial kung fu. I'm all up in your brain now, Neo, swimmin' in your psychology. Your problem is you're capable of love. Whereas my man here turns everything to hate. He even hates you because he can't love like you do. I know this because he made me." He butted his fists together. "My old man and my uncle, two of the best in the business showing the light and dark side of catching feelings. But you know darkness always wins, right?"

"Suck this dick," Mynd Recka said to Vanessa.

The Death Dream Angel made an absurd sight expounding on darkness with a monstrous boner.

"Darkness don't get hurt. It don't fall in love while it's posing undercover as a student. It don't get shocked neither when it walks in on the bitch with some old fat fuck who's grading her on a different curve than the rest of the class reading David Foster Wallace."

"Kurt Vonnegut," Ol' Dirty Wan said.

"My bad. Wrong memory bank." The Death Dream Angel moved behind Vanessa, who snaked half his cock down her throat. "Anyway, darkness don't cry neither when the slut jumps off a bridge three days later. But that's okay, we're gonna make this right." He winked his paintball eye at Ol' Dirty Wan and flashed gold teeth. "We're gonna show your girl how darkness romances."

Ol' Dirty Wan tested the straitjacket. Mynd Recka had charged it with a binding spell. His brother was using humiliation to steal his power. He and his partner mirrored each other slamming Vanessa in ass and mouth. Ol' Dirty Wan was to be the unwilling test audience for a gangbang porno in Third Eyemax.

"Take my big fat novel, girl," the Death Dream Angel said. "*Infinite Jizz*!"

"No, no, *Slaughter Ass Five*." Mynd Recka winked at Ol' Dirty Wan. "Right, brother?"

He watched them smack, slap and jackhammer Vanessa at both ends. A vile caricature of the unfaithful act he had caught the real woman at. "My psychic projections," his brother once boasted, "are nothing to fuck with." The tactic worked despite his cognizance. Victim energy buzzed under Ol' Dirty Wan's straitjacket like a bee swarm. Guilt, betrayal and other deeply buried emotions stung him.

He should not have fallen in love. He should not have shown weakness. He should not have mocked Vanessa when she begged forgiveness. He should not have left her alone the night she killed herself. He should not have argued when the League found his cloaking sigil and extracted him.

"Oh shit, Neo," the Death Dream Angel shouted. "I'm about to bust! *Ch-chick-pow*!"

He should not —

"Witness the strength, brother. Vlad Style, impaling your psyche."

— let Mynd Recka win.

"I forgive you, Vanessa," he said. "If you'll forgive me. Help me." Ol' Dirty Wan's tearful invocation broke the chair straps.

He stood.

"Help me forgive myself for my imperfections. Help me release the pain that binds us. Help me give it all to my brother… with the Franken Style."

His sleeves expanded like balloons. They snapped apart. Gulliver-sized hands shot through the openings. The straitjacket split down the middle, torn by his swelling bulk. Rivets poked from the crown of his head, and his grin made a wound of jagged yellow teeth.

The sperm-soaked automaton with Vanessa's face vanished. Gulliver hands extended, Ol' Franken Dirty advanced on Mynd Recka and the Death Dream Angel. Their flesh opened to the monster like ripe peaches.

Darkness again.

Victory slammed Ol' Dirty Wan back into his dying body. Terminal fever screamed in his nerve cells. His joints throbbed, his hands shook and his teeth chattered a beat that rang to the roof of his skull. He slowed his breaths to conserve oxygen. His muscles strained. The fungus gave him steroid-strength to break free but his grounding cords held firm. His brother had failed to sever them while he tormented Ol' Dirty Wan in illusion.

Heaven and earth qi flushed enemy poison out through his grounding cords.

Ol' Dirty Wan clapped his hands to his temples. The redirected Bobby Digital light burned the zombie toxins in his brain. GODDAMN REIKI FINGAZ, the Death Dream Angel cursed in his mind. Then he said to his brother: "I forgive you, too," and the last he heard was Mynd Recka mutter, "just like that hippie sorceRZA from Nazareth," before consciousness left his body.

The orb expired. Stalks burst through its chest and punched through the casket lid. Ol' Dirty Wan's spirit beat them to the surface and jumped into his astral double by the mound. He watched as the ground shuddered.

The fungus bomb exploded harmlessly, beneath the surface.

"Thank you," he said, to no one and everyone.

If the odds are in your favor, you're fighting the wrong fight.
— The Raekwonomicon

Ol' Dirty Wan climbed onto the wing of the bomber and sat beside Curtis. They watched the sun rise. Morning traffic thickened and shopkeepers opened their doors. A cloaking sigil rendered the two men invisible. Ol' Dirty Wan explained everything — from his insertion in The Crawl to his triumph over Mynd Recka. "The value of nine has a power over my brother similar to the Poetic Wave Principle, but don't ask me to explain it."

Curtis buried his head in his hands when the sorceRZA finished his account.

"I always wanted to write something like this, but you're telling me it's real. Some Michael Moorcock parallel universe shit."

"The fungus turns people into infectious spore bombs. The only way we can stop it is to safely detonate each one."

"By burying them."

"Nine feet deep."

"But it's spread into the cities."

"A lot of digging to be done."

Curtis stood and propped a foot on the plane's port inner engine. "You barely kept your old body from breaking to the surface. How's this going to work with normal people?"

"You dig, I chessbox."

"Sardonicaz and Ol' Dirty Wan," Curtis said. "We sound like a rap group."

Ol' Dirty Wan flashed his new orb's gold front tooth. "The dirtiest."

CHAOS MAGICK FOR SCUMBAGS

Whoa, slow down. You don't want anyone to notice how badly you want this.

Walk casual. Avoid eye contact. Don't look at Mr. Sloane as you ghost your white Nikes through the door.

Ignore Jenny Balfour giving you the stink eye. Stay in character. Remember, you are not you. You are a leaf on the October wind. The breeze sets you down at the desk behind Jenny Balfour's.

As it does every Tuesday and Thursday when your class trades rooms with the eighth graders before third period. This is the high point of your day, but you've got to maintain appearances. Look like you're at a funeral while your classmates stream in.

When the last desk has been taken—by Andy Milner, the straggler—you don't look as if you raced ahead of everyone to secure your seat. You look like one more student waiting for World History to start.

Not that the spoiled brats really see you. As far as your peers are concerned, you're "the Moper"—slant-eyed jerk who spends recess under the fire escape frowning at his shoelaces.

Dreaming of a day when he won't be bullied.

The bell rings third period. "All right, class," Mr. Sloane says.

"Open your books to Chapter Twelve. 'Lessons from Auschwitz.'"

Whatever. Inside, you're smiling. For the next fifty minutes you get a break from being the biggest loser at Our Lady of Devotion Catholic School. You have ceased to become you, remember? You are now a *shaman*.

You're not sure how to pronounce the word, you only know what you've read about it in books about Jim Morrison. A shaman is a magician. You're going to cast a spell to remove the barriers between you and the eighth grader whose desk you have claimed.

Melissa.

You close your eyes and caress the desktop. You press your right knee against the cubbyhole. You picture the items inside its recesses—Bic roller pens, gum erasers, PeeChee folders, loose-leaf paper, fuzzy-headed pencils. Now you have established your sacred space.

You are ready to break on through to the other side. Ever since you saw The Doors' version of "Gloria" on MTV, you fancy yourself an iconoclast and secretly believe you're the Filipino second coming of James Douglas Morrison.

Unfortunately, Melissa doesn't appreciate dead Sixties rock stars. She's into Simon Le Bon. That and the fact that she lives in a gingerbread-looking mansion is why you've resorted to mystical devices. To connect with her, you will have to meet her on a higher plane of existence: You will cast what your smarty-pants adult self would call a *love sigil*.

Up front, Mr. Sloane writes GAS CHAMBER on the black-board. Behind you, on the other side of the wall covered in posters from the television miniseries, *V*—your teacher is obsessed with alien invasions—Melissa is spinning a fuzzy-headed pencil at some lucky student's desk.

Time to set the night on fire.

Intuitively, without words to express the concepts, you know how your love sigil works.

Melissa has carved the first three letters of her name on the upper right-hand corner of her desk. The way you see it, her signature reveals a general wish to be acknowledged. To yourself, you reformulate her wish and declare it as a statement of intention. You trace the letters over and over. They take on a hypnotic quality and become a part gestural, part visual abstraction of your statement. *M-E-L* becomes a sigil, a coded instruction for the hardest working problem-solver in the universe — your subconscious.

Because you're crushing on the girl so badly, you sink into a focused state that commands your mind's hidden depths to manifest your desire.

Soon you are transported from the classroom, from the year 1984, from your white Nikes to the psycho-spiritual plane where class differences and beauty standards do not exist. You become one with Melissa's soul-constituent. You slip inside her etheric skin, feel her soul-nerves, her soul-breath as she carved her nickname.

Maybe it's bullshit, but even a sappy metaphysical fantasy is better than being the Moper.

But, you idiot, you're daydreaming again. Remembering the last time you cast the sigil. You are brought back to the present by Andy Milner, plopping his skinny ass down in front of you for real now. You are wondering when he started wearing aftershave when someone says to you, "Why do you always sit at my desk?"

At this point, we must jump ahead to the Chinese Grocer.

The Chinese Grocer is thin and puffy-eyed and speaks with a thick accent. You won't meet him for another two years. When you do, and he demands you open your backpack and sees the Coke bottles you've rolled inside your stanky freshman P.E. clothes to keep them from shifting, you will feel your scalp light up as if your unwashed hair has ignited in a grease fire.

This is how you feel when you look up at Melissa watching you from the doorway next to Jenny Balfour. As if a Chinese grocer you haven't met yet has grabbed your left hand and said, "I see you in my store again, I cut your finger off!"

"Why do you always sit at my desk?" She repeats.

If only you could tell her. "Because I wanted to transcend social demarcations and connect with your etheric body on the psycho-spiritual plane." But you're years from spitting such abstruseness.

Instead, you can't help but focus on her jaw. The minuscule muscular contractions around her luscious mouth. You realize all that tension stems from rage directed at *you*. To make matters worse, you two are telepathically linked. You've cast your love sigil so many times it's manifesting at the worst possible moment. You are one with Melissa's consciousness, an unwilling Mr. Spock mind melding with the most popular girl in school. You feel Melissa's wrath like a neurotoxin inducing paralysis and scrotum shrinkage in your non-etheric, hormonally triggered body.

Her rage takes on the semblance of a predator inside your skin. In shamanic circles, this beast of prey is known as a *thought-form*. You feel the spawn of your empathy investigating you like a black dog sniffing at bloody butcher paper. Right now, it digs the aroma coming from your heart: The savory scent of unrequited love.

Meanwhile, the object of your affection keeps glaring at you. All you think is, *Please don't treat me like I'm the Moper*.

"I don't want you sitting at my desk," she says.

You can handle predatory thoughtforms and foreshadowings of Chinese grocers, but not this.

"But why?" You say.

"Because you're a scumbag, that's why!"

The beast takes a chomp out of your heart. The bite hurts more than anything you have ever felt in your twelve years and four months on earth.

Scumbag.

You've never heard the word before. But your unconscious mind knows its history back to its 14th-century beginning. Unconsciously, you know its halves have been used to discuss froth, dirt, rejected bits of metal, sugar refining and male contraception. You know the word means "despicable person" in modern use.

You also know it means you're a worthless substance that should be strained like froth through the bag of existence. Because Melissa told you. She knows you better than anyone because of your sigil.

The bell rings third period.

Open your book, scumbag.

❀

High school reaffirms what Melissa taught you. Your superpower is making people despise you on sight. Football players are the meanest, giving you wedgies and throwing your books down the stairs to the boys' restroom. To cope, you sell your *Superman* comic books and buy a weight set. By senior year, you're shoving people aside with a duffel bag bulging with protein powder and unread textbooks.

College is a different story.

You stop lifting weights and start reading textbooks. You wear striped sweaters and designer jeans and speak up in class. You play pranks, crack jokes, anything to get a smile from your peers.

Anything to avoid seeing their jaws clench.

Your inner twelve-year-old still cringes at the sensation of Melissa seething at you. You'll do anything to keep her expression from replicating in the faces around you. But you can't stop progress. Every term, during finals week, Melissa Face infects the entire campus.

During your Advanced Literary Theory exam, you realize you're witnessing the outbreak of a Melissa Face super-virus. Students glaring at the clock and scribbling in their blue books like Jack the Ripper wielding a scalpel. You're infected, too — you'll swallow your tongue if you go another two years with this sickness.

You settle for a bachelor's degree and get a job as a banker.

Now you wear button-down shirts and grab a latte and blueberry muffin on the way to the elevator. You eat lunchroom specials (Taco Salad Tuesdays are the apex of corporate cuisine) and go for happy hour cocktails with your co-workers. You've found your tribe, your 8-to-5 dharma.

Leave it to you to find something wrong.

After two years of empty calories, banging out SWIFT messages, rocking Nautica shirts, burning off pina coladas on the treadmill and yakking around the water cooler ("I think Anita's off the wagon again—she's barely making those bills of lading out before the New York deadline"), you realize you're fucking bored.

You're stealing pens and phone message pads from the back room. You're talking to Tyler in Admin and eying his stapler. You're hoping he'll catch you pilfering it someday and morph into the Chinese Grocer.

This is what happens when you try to blend in.

You are neither a scholar nor a banker.

You are a shaman.

🕸

"You have a thoughtform inside you."

His name is David. He could pass for you on the street. He has your build and features, except for a stronger jaw line and higher cheekbones. He talks like you, too, but with cleaner enunciation and a deadpan voice. He puts out this dangerous vibe, like the panther you dreamed about the night before you found his business card on the sidewalk. The beast sprang at you before you woke up.

You chased David down to a place called Left Hand Acupuncture. You looked at the yellowed scrolls on the walls and the human skull on his desk and thought, *Can this guy help with my jaw ache?* Turns out he can. And more.

His methods go beyond turning you into Pinhead from *Hellraiser*. His muscle testing, for example. You lie on the table and extend your arm toward the ceiling. He has you say a word and pushes against your wrist. When you say words like "home" and "lunch," you resist his pressure. When you say "heart," your shoulder gives out. This is not the levitating sorcery you envisioned based on David's office décor, nor is it scientific, according to skeptics. Yet when he places his hand on your sternum you sense an aha moment coming.

"What happened to you when you were twelve?" He says.

Hard to think back that far with last night's Long Island Iced Teas fuzzing your brain. You say, "Bullies."

David steps back, eclipsing the light in the window. He gives you the 411 on thoughtforms.

"Some people say a thoughtform acts like a computer program. In your case, I see it as a kind of vampire. It began as a desire and deviated into a mind parasite that makes you ashamed of yourself because shame is what feeds it. To control you, it's linked itself to other, external thoughtforms."

"Like what?"

"Any energy emanating from environments where masses of people are trained to think the same thoughts and perform the same motions. Your shame makes you work harder to fulfill your role in these places. But a part of you rebels, which makes you feel even more ashamed. It's a vicious cycle."

That explains your stealing urges.

"How do I get rid of this thing?"

"That depends on if you *want* to get rid of it. The thoughtform has been with you a long time. It could harness great power."

You leave work early, tired and dizzy. You hate yourself for letting this entity get inside you. Correction: You don't hate yourself. That's the entity controlling your emotions.

Then you wonder… how do you know thoughtforms exist? Have you seen one in an X-ray? Do you realize you're taking advice from someone who decorates his office with a human skull? On the other hand, you can't see electromagnetic energy either, but you know it exists.

According to David, the smart thing to do is contact the thoughtform through meditation. Ask its purpose before it turned into a shame vampire.

But you'd rather beat it down for making you hate yourself. For transforming you into a Nordstrom mannequin. Is that you with the Ralph Lauren polo shirt and super-gelled hair scowling at you in your bedroom mirror? Look at what this thing has done.

"You…" Say it.

"*You scumbag.*"

There it is. Thoughtform, thy name is Scumbag.

Now that you've spoken its name, you taste its power on your adrenal palate. Slap-to-the-face flavor with a road-rage finish. "Scumbag," you spit at the mirror again. Another rush like someone shoving you, challenging you to fight back. "Scumbag. Scumbag." The chant has you shaking, slipping into a trance state. God knows what, but you're onto something.

"Scumbag." You shout the word like a crazed televangelist. "*Scumbagscumbagscumbagscumbag.*" You scream the word so loud your upstairs neighbor turns down her housecleaning music, "Sweet Child O' Mine," to hear you scorch your lungs Axl Rose-style.

Your instincts tell you to punch the mirror, add blood to this impromptu inner housecleaning spell. Your reflection turns black and stops you.

The shadow clone extends its arms like Superman flying and lowers them halfway. You fall to your knees and watch the mirror being liquefy while Slash wah-wahs into his guitar solo. Are you scared of this protean upgrade of yourself that you've somehow manifested with your screaming? Would you prefer to squander your youth sending telexes and delivering interoffice mail? Fuck no.

The black goo runs down the mirror and spills onto the carpet. It flows up your khaki pants and vanishes into the cotton like spilled grape juice under a Bounty paper towel. You are the quicker picker upper of something leaked from another plane of existence.

There on your knees, drooling like an overstimulated mutt, you see your reflection reappear in the mirror. You look like shit.

Talk about an awkward origin story. What have you become?

Quit the bank.

Stock shelves at Sticky Mart.

Bloat up on Rice-A-Roni and Cup O'Noodles soup.

Write a book.

Write two.

Get a name in the small presses.

Get a call from a literary agent.

Roll with the big dogs.

Strike a deal with a film studio.

Hit the talk shows.

Radio shows.

Award shows.

For the new book *and* the movie.

Get a mansion.

Buy a gym franchise.

Start a fitness craze.

Don't mention the Test/Tren/Anadrol you cycled to gain twenty pounds of muscle.

Go on tour.

Make demands such as: "I will only read onstage if I am allowed to dress like a panther with my balls hanging out."

Acquire the world's largest titan beetle collection.

Punch a reviewer in the throat for calling *Sad Bone Prison* a suckfest.

Settle out of court.

Break stuff.

Hurt people.

Defy your editors.

You're worth millions being a scumbag.

This is how you get famous, but it omits the coolest part.

After you tell David about the mirror incident, he introduces you to chaos magic—the "left hand path" alluded to in his business name. He gives you books with titles like *Chaos and Sorcery* and *Mysteria Magica*. You procure the basics: Altar, candles, gemstones, Thoth tarot deck. You try breathing exercises, divinations, evocations.

Getting witchy with it pays off.

You leave the heavy lifting—such as mentally manipulating a New York agent—to David's coven, the Order of the Iron Spider. Except for David, you never get face time with your occult benefactors. They contact you through a dream channel in your subconscious opened by the black goo.

You hire David full-time to protect you from enemies protoplasmic and ectoplasmic. Because haters will hate in *all* dimensions.

At times you wonder if he hasn't created a network of Davids —or David-like entities—to assist him. You'll see him lurking in a corner only to turn and find him standing beside you. At your reading events, you'll see stick figures riding the audience wave like crowd-surfing shadow puppets.

You try not to dwell on such oddities, knowing they're in your favor. You stay in your lane, nailing fangirls, waging author beefs and creating a brand based on vitriol and overwrought swagger. This is your new superpower since you duked it out with your thoughtform in the mirror: The more you shit on people, the more they love you.

Maybe not the waitress you stiffed on the tip, but the legions of numbskulls who make you a household name. Who laud you for being an explosive social critic, "a tempestuous Adonis who spews invective like a flamethrower." You know the whole thing sucks, commodifying the shittiest parts of your personality in a capitalist society that rewards unruly behavior. But hey, you're rich, and the Melissas of the world are begging you to sit at their desk. Men too, much to your annoyance sometimes.

"You're hot, dude, you're like Hunter S. Thompson if he worked out with John Cena," a bear tells you at a signing. The mountainous, garlic-breathed bastard passes on the *Snout Full of Filth* T-shirt that pairs at a discount with the hardcover.

He's partly right. You cycle steroids like Thompson snorted

coke. But the Doctor only manipulated reality in a psychotropic sense. You osmosed the black goo, you brought in energies that converted your self-loathing into a love spell over millions... and you have no idea what checks are being drawn on your spiritual bank account.

This gnaws at the lapsed Catholic in you, so you up the bad behavior to escape your unease. When you mug a man for his Dr. Dre headphones, you know you're in pilfering mode again but with the wrecking ball mentality that makes you a counter-culture authority. You accept a plea bargain and the video of you reconciling with the victim—signing his copy of *Snout Full of Filth*—goes viral.

About the affair, one thinkpiece writer says: "In life as in art, the notorious author of *Sad Bone Prison* takes a bare-knuckle approach to delivering his message: He's pissed off, and so should you be." In other words, keep punchin', bro.

Today, you could beat the Chinese Grocer with a fire extinguisher and steal all the Coke in his store and people would cheer. "His Shakespearean rage," they would say. "His apocalyptic genius," they would say. You're like the crook in the *Twilight Zone* episode who finds out Hell is getting everything he asks for.

This is the love you asked for when you paid homage to the shadow figure in the mirror, but it's not what you want. Under the steroid acne canvas that is your skin, you are still the Moper.

You've embarked on a hero's journey to erase that—from English major nerd to corporate wage slave to anti-establishment literary icon. You end up where you started, though.

Bored.

You would give David anything. He keeps it old school, though. Same yellowed scrolls on the walls, same human skull on his desk.

"You could at least get a new chair," you whine whenever he treats you. The Shaker chair's creak and sway make you feel trapped in 1997, stiff-jawed and stapler-obsessed, a real-life recidivist doing time in a *Sad Bone Prison*.

Even the man's face stays the same. You attribute his sickening youthfulness to martial arts and an aversion to anything fun. Face it, you resent David for making you feel like a failed version of yourself… though it's not his fault he resembles you.

(Why have neither of you talked about this? Why in the rivers of ink that have been poured in your name has no one pointed this out?)

Your dead ringer is watching you like a demented Stanley Kubrick character, psychically scanning your meridians. He says: "Are you worried about someone?"

"I don't know… I dreamed I was attacked by a panther last night." The same one that dream-jumped you the night before you first met David. The man straightens. You're about to get the 411 on dream symbols.

You jump in first. "According to the Internet, the dream means people are saying bad things about me. Well, no shit. They still buy my books and go to my readings. You're there to shut down the ones who spring their ratty crushes on me at the point of a gun."

David chuckles. "True enough."

"I hate them. All of them… everyone who has something to say about me. I hate the pseudo-intellectual gibberish people use to justify their addiction to me. I hate anyone who uses words like 'zeitgeist' and 'anomie.' I hate that everyone's become a walking thinkpiece."

You clench your fists on your thighs. The chair groans.

"They make me want to take a bath, all the bullshit flooding through my phone and my laptop and my eyes and ears every day. You remember when we were in Japan a few years ago? I couldn't read the signs or understand a word people said. It was heavenly. But oh, 'boo-hoo,' people say. 'You're hating us all the way to the bank, you hypocrite.' They have no idea who I am, but they rattle off dissertations about me. Fans are the stupidest people in the world, David. And I keep getting more of them."

You wonder who's grumpier now, David's geriatric chair or

the crank sitting in it. But the flamethrower's on and roasting celebrity culture with grandiose elan (another word you detest).

"The soul-sucking cabbage-heads," you say. "The soft-bellied, privileged, rancid piles of malignancy. The back-biting dilettantes! 'Boo-hoo,' they say, 'you narcissistic hack, you hypermasculine, socially clueless, hokum-spewing…'"

David's watching you as if you're a child pouting over their dinner.

"You need a vacation," he says.

"What I need to do is go back to the beginning, before I got famous. I need to scare myself. It used to terrify me putting myself out in front of people. But now it doesn't matter." A bird, a hawk maybe, swoops past your mansion's north tower outside the window.

David rises, blocking the window. His posture reminds you of your long-ago shadow clone.

"You're overworked," he says. "Depleted. When that happens, your ancestry kicks in. You come from a warrior culture, same as me. When I'm run down, I'll catch myself fighting adversaries in my mind that represent the things I can't control. But I have a wooden dummy to absorb my anger. Weightlifting's different. It's chimerical. You're always chasing gains to outgun the enemies in your head. Basically, you're still fighting the kids who bullied you. You need to disrupt this pattern."

Before you can argue, David tells you to remove your shoes and socks and get on his table. He works his needle magic.

All the while you're thinking: *Disrupt the pattern…*

For all your issues, you're nothing like Gordon Pierce. This idea scares the shit out of you.

Yet your fear grounds you in reality. Sharpens your senses. Gives you nightmares. They offer a way back to yourself… a return to the beginning.

It's not as if you're causing anything to happen. If you had that power, you would make men like Gordon Pierce spontaneously combust before they got the first shot off. It's not as if you're greasing the wheels of American gun massacres, either. You're simply slipping your brand into tragedies before they happen... the opposite of good product placement.

Back to the beginning, then. To your bedroom. 1,500 square feet of sacred space. Circle of power drawn on the floor with salt —check. Red candles placed inside the pentagram—check. Book of Shadows—check. Mojo bag filled with calamus root, sigils and dried blood drops—check. $46,000 dollar Chinese famille rose center bowl containing .308 tracer round and Pierce photo—check. Bath ritual—check. Anointment in Lucifer oil—check.

Occult lock-and-load montage completed. Initiate spell sequence.

Grab the mojo bag. Enter the circle.

You're nude because clothes absorb unwanted energy before a ritual. The way you see it, real magicians don't wear robes, anyway. Those are for Ren Faire dorks.

Visualize Mr. Sloane's classroom. There he is, tapping papers down at his table. There's Jenny Balfour giving you the stink eye. Set your ass down at Melissa's desk. Feel the cold wood grain. Tune in to the chatter of students pouring in. Check out the backpacks on the wall hooks. And the posters on the back wall—the one that stands out shows a fleet of flying saucers superimposed by a red V in a street-style graffiti font. Mr. Sloane's obsession with the Eighties television miniseries, *V*... where reptilian aliens invade Earth wearing human disguises and rust-colored jumpsuits.

Hmm. Why does the poster say "The Original Miniseries" when the program hasn't been remade yet? No matter, creativity trumps period authenticity here. You're priming yourself for spell-work with a powerful emotion.

Shame brings pain. Pain produces anger. Anger provides focus.

Whiff of aftershave. Right on cue, Andy Milner plops down in front of you.

Here it comes. Your childhood crush, so fired up she goes straight for the punch line:

"BECAUSE YOU'RE A SCUMBAG, THAT'S WHY!"

Scumbag

Scumbag

Scumbagscumbagscumbag

End scene.

Fade to black.

Correction: Red.

Like a spray-painted V. V for violence. For victims. Not "Visitors" from outer space.

Pierce. His haunted face in the photo in the Chinese bowl. Embed the image in your mind's eye. Run fictionalized gunman reel. Pierce inspecting the sixteen guns he's smuggled into the apartment-style hotel room where he lives. Pierce wearing your *Snout Full of Filth* T-shirt. Pierce snapping a selfie with you.

Now blur his face. Picture the generic shooter in his bedroom. He's admiring his rifles and ammo and magazines... and the one bookcase filled with your novels and merchandise. Zoom in on him. See your memory-induced anger as a hulking, V-for-violence red hammer splitting his skull open.

Now shoot black goo into his exposed brains. Repeat while squeezing the mojo bag: *"Kill for me. Kill for me. Kill for me."* Make Sniper McGee grandfather YOU into his vision of glory. When he commits mass murder in your name, he will do so like a rabid sports fan waving a foam finger... one that gets off 20 to 90 shots in ten seconds or less.

Go, Team Scumbag, go!

And when the Gordon Pierces blaze their way into headlines while wearing your T-shirts, you'll neither condemn nor condone their actions. When asked how you feel about each new tragedy, you'll obfuscate from your mansion like the CEO of a secret corporation that rakes in billions from mass shooting attacks.

You'll blame the drug companies, parents, inadequate mental health care for the death tolls amassed by disgruntled men who want fame, and, apparently, to be validated by you—the poster boy for pretentious aggro.

You'll finally go too far. Millions of consumers will reevaluate your success. Or will they? Will your love spell protect you? Will people in the street shrug off your problematic association with mass murderers? Will thinkpiece writers call your song and dance "self-defense in a volatile social milieu?"

Spell sequence completed. Initiate laughing fit. You can't close a ritual without a banishing, not after working heady magic like this.

Hahahahahahahahahaaaaaaaa

HAAAhahahahahahahahaaaaaaaa

BwaaaHAAAAAAhahahahahahahaaaaaaaa

Stop.

System warning: Your magic may be infected. How else did you get to the walkway outside the north tower just now?

Someone has hacked your blood spell.

❀

You know this is not your rooftop. You haven't left your bedroom. But you are stuck—worse, *paralyzed* in this illusion. All you can do is keep calm and accept that you are freeze-framed and still naked. At least you've got a nice view.

The koi pond, animal topiaries, David's carriage house. Blue sky laced with contrails. Downtown twenty minutes away, swarming with ant people. They're waiting at traffic lights, slouching in cubicles, stepping off curbs into their phones' social media feeds... illusions with the illusion.

Thank God you're not one of them, you think, and realize you're intellectualizing a dire situation. You're in deep shit. You exploited your sacred fluid to enact a kind of death wish. Not that you're a demonologist, but you've seen enough to know your blood is the sexiest thing you can hustle for a change of outcomes and will entice the sort of beings that have gray, badly sutured skin in movies but only truly manifest as flashes of infernal torment inside your mind.

This is what you wanted though, right? You cast the blood spell on your own because you've never taken an extreme risk.

You've always walked the tightrope with David's net beneath you.

Whatever comes next is the price you pay for trying to burn down everything you've built since you watched your reflection liquefy in a mirror. The thinkpiece cliché that finally means something… your catastrophic personal truth.

Right now, your meat vessel is probably pissing all over your brand-new wool Berber carpet. You might escape this trap by meditating on its median nerve and making it wiggle its fingers. You've heard that helps with sleep paralysis. You're not asleep, though. You're caught somewhere between a trance and the conscious state you were working toward when someone or something hacked into your banishing ritual. Still, it can't hurt to try and move your fingers.

Nothing. It's as if your physical body has been anesthetized.

The hackers must have picked up your signal. Eight dark-robed figures glitter into place in front of the battlements. You should have known. David beams in last, wearing his red robe signifying authority. He rises in the air until he floats several feet above his cabalistic *Star Trek* security team. Like the others, his face remains hidden inside his hood.

You think maybe the coven doesn't know this is a bad time to dream-conference. Then, despite their manner of entrance, you realize how freaky everyone looks. You're used to seeing them in their B-movie-style dream setting, gathered by candle light around a black-draped altar. In this homier illusion, the Order of the Iron Spider looks creepily legit, less like Satanists in a Hammer horror film and more like unearthly beings who can smoke motherfuckers literally, with smoke.

Knowing David, there is a point to this disruption. This isn't a last-minute project update. It's an intervention by protectors who know you're making their job harder.

"You should have taken a vacation." David rises higher, a mash-up of Superman and Anton LaVey. "But maybe this is for the best."

In the real world he's probably also naked, along with the other guys you've never met projecting their avatars on your supposed rooftop. Thinking of them as raw, fleshy beings does nothing to diminish the illusion, however. The coven is calling you out despite the countless shady spells it has cast at your behest. Apparently it draws the line at forming marketing tie-ins with rampaging shooters.

David spreads his hands in a Jesusy gesture. A strand of blood shoots from each palm. The funky stigmata fluids arc down to the walkway and paint a figure three feet long. It looks like a pyramid with squished hearts inside it formed by lines that extend outward to three surrounding discs. The other coven members spread their hands also and squirt blood strands onto the figure.

David chants: "Travelers from the stars, I invoke you. Travelers from the stars, I summon you. Travelers from the stars, I conjure you." To the west, an immense black disc appears in the sky. "Come forth, travelers from the stars, and manifest yourselves."

Now the speeding vessel obscures the sky. Its undersurface blurs with a dream-sequence effect. The hull turns submarine-gray. Structural details dream-ripple in wherever you look. Welding seams, flashing lights, modular house-like structures and tubes that presumably fire humongous lasers... the craft is molding itself to your visual of how an alien starship should appear. Even though it's a phantasm, you don't know how it fits into David's intervention yet. Stop arming it with your eyeballs!

Meanwhile, back on the rooftop, the coven vanishes. Only its high priest remains, still hovering. You step toward him. Suddenly you're warm, despite your nakedness. The temperature has risen because of the mega-saucer trapping the earth's heat.

You haven't felt heat since you tumbled into this illusion. This can only mean one thing.

You're not in an illusion anymore.

As if on a moving walkway in the air, the two of you shoot off toward the city. Able to move around again, you feel god-like, zipping over highways packed with stopped ant cars and ant people wondering where the sky went. A cool feeling until you recall you have something to do with the weird night quality that's fallen over the land.

"You told me to disrupt the pattern," you say, now hovering above the outskirts of the city center. "Is this what you had in mind?"

"I told you you're still fighting with people you haven't seen in thirty years," David answers. "Drawing on your warrior ancestry—avoiding your pain by lashing out at phantoms. Your rage threatens the coven's existence. It's eating us slowly, like a cancer."

He glances up at the spaceship. A shuttle emerges from a landing bay positioned above central downtown.

"So the Order of the Iron Spider has chosen to redirect your energies. We've brought forth an outsider more powerful than any army on earth. It's up to *you* what happens when these beings reveal their purpose. Will they be friends or enemies? Models of a new way or instruments of your same old rancor? Dozens of mother ships are hovering over cities across the globe, ready to act out your impulses of love or hate. We're interested to see if you can change your pattern or if you'll display your usual proclivity to cause harm."

Is David serious? Is he really putting the planet's fate in your hands? You, who mugged someone for their Dr. Dre headphones?

Are you really naked, really fucking naked, hundreds of feet in the air, watching a shuttle descend from a flying saucer that looks as if it warped into the atmosphere from an Eighties television miniseries?

Do you really have to choose between utopia and Armageddon?

"But why?" You whine to your only means of avoiding an Icarus-like fall to the traffic interchange below. "Because I'm pissed off? I don't have the power to be a threat to the coven. You're way stronger than I am."

"I'm not. You created me. You made me so I could remake

you. I made the coven so we could help you rise to your true power. We didn't think your power was to be a festering, sophomoric, dead horse-beating dick."

Whoa.

You're so fixated on your tabloid lifestyle that you've never bothered to question David's static nature. Now you know why he never ages. He's a physically realized product of your imagination. So are the saucer people, the shadow clone, the black goo... they're constructs of your mind that have crossed over into the realm of substance.

As a plot twist, this would never fool your readers. But as a confession from your made-up self to your actual self? In your current predicament?

Worth repeating: Whoa.

"All right, so I'm a dick," you say. "But you don't need to punish the world for it. Even if I had Superman's powers, I wouldn't do something like this. I wouldn't literally kill everyone."

David says, "Let's see if you're speaking the truth."

"Fine, then. The 'Visitors' are our friends. For real, not like in the show which you're totally ripping off."

Zipping along on the magical walkway again. Toward the plaza where the shuttle starts landing. SWAT teams stand ready while riot police form a perimeter against the swelling crowd. Police Cessnas and news helicopters hover above the circus, which includes stilt walkers and a deejay playing Public Enemy's "Bring the Noise" on the roof of an insurance building. Thank God no one seems to notice the Ren Faire wizard and naked celebrity floating above the cops and news crews... although you two would complement the Ringling Brothers slash MTV vibe.

The shuttle lands. On its starboard side, a bay door opens. Someone emerges.

❀

From your position, you can't hear the "Visitor's" speech. But you'll soon know if the alien ambassador fails to charm the locals.

Beside you, David folds his wizard robe arms. "Hopefully, your words reflect what's in your heart," he says.

Congratulations on creating someone who sounds like a cross between Gandalf and a Roxette song. David lost his cliché filter the moment he outed himself as your externalized imaginary chief assistant. Will humanity live to see another day? Listen to your heart…

"Crazy." You picture Melissa in the crowd. You haven't thought of her in years. "All this because of what some girl called me in grade school."

In your Cruella de Vil version of Melissa, she is standing on a street corner waving her cigarette holder and shouting at her assistants. *"I don't like those aliens landing their spaceship in our city… BECAUSE THEY'RE SCUMBAGS, THAT'S WHY!!!"*

"Fuck what anyone else thinks," you say. "Melissa Horak was a bitch. A stuck-up, snitty rich cunt."

"No," David says.

"You don't get to tell me no."

"This isn't happening because you were mistreated. This is happening because of what sparked between your mind and reality when you chose to believe a petty insult."

"Oh, I see. You're telling me to stop obsessing over ancient history. The 'Eighties nostalgia' thing is played out, right?"

David shakes his head. "Same old rancor…"

Condescending fucknut. But face it, wouldn't you rather be like him? He's beside you, but he might as well be hovering in outer space, he's so Zen and fairy-like, so sickeningly composed. He's like the spiritual leader who came from the world's worst parent, the lotus that grew from filth. You can't even stop his clichés from taking root inside you.

You can't stop this from happening, either. You can't stop the "Visitors" from fulfilling whatever urge they're linked to in your Roxette heart.

Then the idea hits. You created the Gandalf wannabe responsible for this mess. You can create another entity to clear a way out of it… a spiritual familiar in the form of an inner voice. He'll have to warp your concept of time if you're to rise to David's challenge. Before the "Visitor's" speech ends, this familiar has to help you relive key events and understand them without turbocharging your adrenaline secretions. You'll never know kindness if you're always wanting to wail on bullies.

Say it: "Narrative-familiar, I invoke thee. Narrative-familiar, I summon thee. Narrative-familiar, I conjure thee. Come forth, narrative-familiar, and manifest thyself."

Consider it done. Here we are, ready to help you disrupt the pattern. Change what's in your heart.

Listen. We're turning the clock back. We're in Mr. Sloane's classroom again.

Whoa, slow down...

❀

So that's it. We're all caught up. For the first time since we started this narrative, we are in the actual present. Live and up-to-the-minute. Judging by the cheering in the streets, our "instant therapy" worked.

Maybe you don't want to hug trees and talk to clouds at this moment, but you're feeling mellower than you have in years. You've reaffirmed you're a whole being, someone who has needs and dreams and feelings. Admit it, you're even feeling love for yourself, the theme of your secretly favorite song by Whitney Houston: "The Greatest Love of All."

So the "Visitors" come in peace. Everyone lives to see another day. But what about us? Your Johnny-on-the-spot when it comes to warp-speed emotional healing? Don't we deserve to stick around, too?

Going forward, think of us more as a sports announcer than a therapist inside your head. We'll give you the down and distance before the quarterback throws the pass. We'll call up the stats when the wide receiver fumbles the ball. After all, you invoked us to give color commentary on your life's journey. There's no reason we can't keep going.

We know you better than anyone, even David. We know your deepest motivations. Let the world's leading experts on you tell your story. If you get tired of us, bind us to the other monologues droning in the back of your mind. Ignore us like we're mental chatter. Don't send us back to your subconscious!

We'll take your silence for approval.

And now back to you, narrative-familiar. What's the scene from your aerial viewpoint over downtown?

It's looking good. A woman emerges from the crowd, attended by men-in-black types. She embraces the "Visitor." Hand in hand, the two dignitaries step to the center of the plaza and wave toward the multitudes. Even from this far up, you can hear people shouting and applauding this historic alliance between two worlds.

Spectators are shooting confetti cannons. Blowing party horns. Waving twisting balloons. It's a scene reminiscent of New Year's Eve in Times Square. As if the deejay thinks so too, "Auld Lang Syne" starts playing on the roof of the insurance building. Some rowdy element is setting off firecrackers.

Hold the phone, those aren't firecrackers—they're shots from a semi-automatic rifle!

The alien ambassador goes down… the civic leader and her bodyguards—down! Security guards from both sides are racing into the gunfire. Another "Visitor" down! Another man in black down! And the shooting continues—no one is safe!

Ambulances and fire trucks are crawling through the congestion. People are hunkering down or stampeding in all directions. What began as a friendly exchange between two worlds has become a close encounter of the worst kind. Deejay, shut the music off—

The shooter has stopped to reload.

What a time for a shooting massacre. Not that there's ever a time to gun down innocent people… but this Gordon Pierce copycat may have awakened a sleeping giant from the stars.

The gunman has started firing again. A stilt walker's been hit. Why in hell is he still on stilts? This is no time to be weird, folks. It's a flood of terror down there. It's almost impossible for the cop cars and armored vehicles to cut through the mobs of fleeing people at every intersection.

Meanwhile, police planes are circling a bank tower on Fifth Avenue. Have they spotted the gunman? Yes! A SWAT team is pulling up by the front entrance. They're storming the building. This should all be over with soon.

What's this? More alien guards are pouring out of the shuttle in the plaza. They're carrying what look like tank guns with chainsaw grips. The "Visitors" are using their superior technology to back up our police units. Thank the stars, literally thank the stars they're taking our side against the shooter.

No—they're firing on the bank tower!

Streaks of blue lightning… a burst of smoke… the top of the tower explodes in a ball of flame! The mushrooming fireball consumes the police planes! A column of black smoke is billowing from the burning prison of glass and granite. Hundreds of people must be trapped on the upper floors—and the great gray saucer hovers mercilessly above the carnage!

All through the streets, people have stopped dead in their tracks. Fire trucks are having a terrible time cutting through the horror-stricken throngs.

As for the alien troopers, no one dares to retaliate. They're boarding the shuttle. They're lifting off. They're getting away. No, jet fighters are roaring in from the south. They're firing on the shuttle! The bullets are bouncing off some kind of deflector shield! We have just declared war against the "Visitors!"

Now the bank tower is collapsing! Fifty-six floors are crashing down! The cloud of dust and debris could swallow Godzilla! It's rolling through the streets engulfing everything in its path!

Joseph Conrad said it best: "The horror! The horror!"

We are witnessing the fall of civilization… this is just a taste of what the aliens have in store for us. We attacked them. We exercised our right to bear arms against them in maniacal ways.

Forget moral distinctions. Forget the differences between a gunman and an air strike. There is no morality in the streets, only blood and terror. The deejay may as well switch the music to Public Enemy's "Countdown to Armageddon."

Why call the plays anymore? We're putting down our headsets. We're going off the air. You and us, we need to talk.

❦

We know what you're thinking. You're not to blame for this. You're telling yourself the gunman would have shot the victims regardless of your blood spell. Never mind that he surfaced because of the "Visitors" or that your right-hand man projected the aliens from your memory.

You're also processing what it means that David has just now retired into thin air. He's absorbed back into you, his job complete. He initiated you into a world of infinite possibilities… a.k.a. the left hand path.

Now here you are, floating under no external influence high above the city. Until now, you thought only comic-book heroes and freaks like David could defy gravity. Speaking of your mentor, now that you've absorbed him you know everything he knows—most importantly, that he wanted you to gain *immortality*. Such was the intention he sigilized with the coven's blood.

To get the ball rolling, he whipped up an unbeatable enemy. Then he merged into you to awaken you to the god-like potential your magical creations have steadily expanded. Now all you have to do is prove to yourself you're like a Timex watch: You can take the "Visitors'" licking and keep on ticking. Be the last man standing after seven billion people have been slaughtered by the aliens and *snap*!

The artist formerly known as "the Moper" inherits the earth.

Talk about ruthless. David sacrificed the human race to manifest your transcendence of death. He tricked you into handling your emotional baggage to keep you from interfering and to purify you for World War *V*, the vehicle of your ascension.

You're chaos magic's answer to the Man of Steel… supreme… invincible… flooded with self-awareness and completely upgraded now. No force in the universe can harm you.

You're trying not to revel in these disclosures, but it's hard not to smile when you're descending into clouds of smoke and dust as easily as you would ride a down escalator into the Macy's perfume department. Sirens and screams reach your ears like distant Muzak. You're beaming your X-ray vision down into the smoking mounds of devastation and sure enough, you spot a torso. It's buried under limbs and handbags and computer hardware and concrete and its stomach has fused with the frame of a baby stroller, but you can identify the *Snout Full of Filth* T-shirt its trigger-happy owner had been wearing.

What else can you do with your new superpowers?

Whatever you discover, keep us in the picture. You need us. Going forward, think of us more as an adviser than a sports announcer inside your head. Someone who can guide you through the monumental task of starting the world over. Otherwise, can you imagine the havoc you might wreak in a post-apocalyptic, shitfucked wasteland?

Of course, you can. That's the problem.

Listen, we know there's still good inside you. We know you didn't set out to leave your mark by turning the earth into a funeral pyre. In a way, you were duped by your creations... but you've found a steroid made for ultimate endurance and you'll do whatever it takes to maximize the gains from it.

Even if it means acting like a coward. Not lifting a finger to help your own people. We get it: As much as this part sucks, it's the last step to fulfilling your destiny. For David's plan to succeed, you've got to let the world burn.

You can't stop there, though. After the destroyers have left, you have to rebuild. Use your superpowers to heal the soil. Repopulate the planet (perhaps an even bigger task than conjuring the "Visitors!") Grow a new Earth Community. Be responsible. Be decent. Who knows? Maybe this is your next step to achieving full-fledged godhood.

Keeping such thoughts in mind is why you need us. We're your voice of reason, your source of wisdom. Are you listening?

Don't banish us. Don't
Hahahahahahahahaaaaaaaa
banish
HAAAhahahahahahahaaaaaaaa
us
BwaaaHAAAAAAhahahahahahahaaaaaaaa
Don't send us back
You need us
Don't send
You need

Narrative-familiar, I thank you for your service.
But I don't need you anymore.
I don't need anyone.

STORIES BEHIND THE STORIES

This is a Horror Book

One day I came across a large hardcover book propped against the outer wall of a Plaid Pantry. It was called *Bruce L. Gibb, a farmboy's stories* (sic). My curiosity about Mr. Gibb lost out to my paranoid fantasy that whoever left the book there smeared poo on the back of it. So I kept walking, but recreated the book in a horror story about two drunk guys watching movies together. No story ends well whenever two drunk guys watch movies together. Except for this one, sort of.

Skype Me at the Public Library

I like this story, even though George calls my goatee "patchy and pubic-hairy." George is kind of a dick. But he gives an accurate account of what happened at the town library.

The Haddonfield Hit Squad

Of the stories collected here, this was the most fun to write. My wife really has a thing about man-love, and a bunch of people on social media really argued about how Michael Myers should hold a knife. Now that I'm no longer made of flesh and blood, I miss my wife and I even miss social media. Okay, now I'm depressed. On to the next story…

Notes on a Cosmic Horrorcore Album

…definitely one of my bleaker pieces. Minus Professor Butler's intro, it was originally published on Thomas Ligotti Online. Speaking of TLO, I cured my online porn addiction by performing a sex magick ritual that involved perusing the website for twenty-four hours. Fueled by aphrodisiacs too weird to reveal, I pored over articles, interviews, forum threads and members' avatars until I could no longer contain my lust for the malignant uselessness of existence. If you're addicted to online porn or just sick of the usual fare, give this cure a try.

Catch You on the Flip Side

Now that you know way too much about me, you're probably thinking this story is autobiographical. It's not. I don't have a monobrow.

O Mother Goddess, Where Art Thou?

I wrote the first draft in twenty minutes. Then I took over a year to flesh out the story between other projects. This is my homage to Samuel Beckett and an attempt to deal with losing an actual mother goddess—Cheryl Annette Muir. I miss you, Mom.

Hood Sigil

I really hate those signs that say "Drive Like Your Kids Live Here." This poem is actually a sigil with the intention to destroy them all.

The Raekwonomicon

I'd like to say I wrote this while channeling the spirit of Ol' Dirty Bastard. The truth is I was invited to submit to an anthology dedicated to the Wu Tang Clan called *This Book Ain't Nuttin to Fuck With*. I did some research (I'd never listened to the rap group before), became a fan and wrote this pulpy tale of mystical kung fu fights and parasitic fungi. To top it all off, the spirit of ODB possessed me on the day the anthology was released. He sent me to a strip club and made me give Brandi enough dolla dolla bills to cover her next term's tuition.

Chaos Magick for Scumbags

You're reliving your youth in the heat of creation. You're sweating at your keyboard, thinking, "Who the hell will publish an eight-thousand-word story in present tense, second person?" Fortunately, you run into a publisher you know at a writing convention. He asks if you're working on anything. That night, you draw a pentagram on the floor of your room, masturbate and pray for a book contract through the powers of Satan. (You have fun masturbating even though the Prince of Darkness ignores you.) Months later, you tell all your social media friends that your book will be published. Then you pull down your pants and pray to Satan for good reviews and even better sales. Why? Because you're the lowliest of scumbags—a writer.

ACKNOWLEDGMENTS

A big thanks to the following people/entities for their support, wisdom, inspiration and affection:

Kara Picante, David Tircuit, Lucas Mangum, Brendan Vidito, Shane Bitterling, Jay Jacobs, James Butler, Christoph Paul, Leza Cantoral, Sam Richard, Nihilism Revised, Bizarro-Con, my air guitar peeps (especially the Farnans for showing me Black's Beach), Iggy Sancho, mom, dad, Dede and Brian.

Also a shout-out to my man George and the Un-Barbees. This book wouldn't exist without you guys.

Charles Austin Muir was an author, hip-hop artist and sorcerer before all the weird shit happened. He wrote a book called *Bodybuilding Spider Rangers and Other Stories*. He also contributed to many magical anthologies, including *Peel back the Skin*, *18 Wheels of Horror*, *Strange Behaviors* and *This Book Ain't Nuttin to Fuck With*. He loved watching horror and action movies, spooning his dog Iggy and crushing post-Derlethian emcees in Lovecraftian rap battles. He hopes you'll start reading this horror book all over again.

George John Wayne Kuato was a personal trainer before all the weird shit happened. He enjoyed hiking, romantic comedies and artisanal cheeses. He wishes you would put down this horror book and do something amazing. His resemblance to Charles Austin Muir is purely coincidental.

ALSO BY CLASH BOOKS

www.ingramcontent.com/pod-product-compliance
Lightning Source LLC
Jackson TN
JSHW080203141224
75386JS00029B/1020